Nora Roberts

The Pride of

Jared MacKade

Mills & Boon, an imprint of Harlequin (UK) Limited,
Eton House, 18-24 Paradise Road, Richmond, Surrey TW9 1SR

© Nora Roberts 1995

ISBN: 978 0 263 90455 0

029-0313

Harlequin (UK) policy is to use papers that are natural, renewable and recyclable products and made from wood grown in sustainable forests. The logging and manufacturing processes conform to the legal environmental regulations of the country of origin.

Printed and bound by
CPI Group (UK) Ltd, Croydon, CR0 4YY

For women with a past

Prologue

The woods echoed with war whoops and running feet. Troops were fully engaged in the battle, peppering the fields beyond the trees with sporadic shelling. The day rang with the crash of weapons and the cries of the wounded.

Already dozens of lives had been lost, and the survivors were out for blood.

Leaves, still lush and green from the dying summer, formed a canopy overhead, allowing only thin, dusty beams of sunlight to trickle through. The air was thick and humid and carried the rich scent of earth and animal in its blistering heat.

There was no place Jared MacKade was happier than in the haunted woods.

He was a Union officer, a captain. He got to be captain because, at twelve, he was the oldest, and it was his right. His troops consisted of his brother Devin, who, being ten, had to be content with the rank of corporal.

Their mission was clear. Annihilate the Rebels.

Because war was a serious business, Jared had plotted out his strategy. He'd chosen Devin for his troops because Devin could follow orders. Devin was also a good thinker.

And Devin was a vicious take-no-prisoners hand-to-hand fighter.

Rafe and Shane, the other MacKade brothers, were ferocious fighters too, but they were, Jared knew, impulsive. Even now, they were racing through the woods, whooping and hollering, while Jared waited patiently in ambush.

"They're going to separate, you watch," Jared muttered as he and Devin hunkered down in the brush. "Rafe figures on drawing us out and clobbering us." Jared spit, because he was twelve and spitting was cool. "He doesn't have a military mind."

"Shane doesn't have a mind at all," Devin put in, with the expected disdain of brother for brother.

They grinned over that, two young boys with disheveled black hair and handsome faces that were grimy with dirt and sweat. Jared's eyes, a cool grassy green, scanned the woods. He knew every rock, every stump, every beaten path. Often he came here alone, to wander or just to sit. And to listen. To the wind in the trees, the rustle of squirrels and rabbits. To the murmur of ghosts.

He knew others had fought here, died here. And it fascinated him. He'd grown up on the Civil War battlefield of Antietam, Maryland, and he knew, as any young boy would, the maneuvers and mistakes, the triumphs and tragedies of that fateful day in September 1862.

A battle that had earned its place in history as the bloodiest day of the Civil War was bound to tug at the imagination of a young boy. He had combed every foot of the battlefield with his brothers, played dead in Bloody Lane, raced through his own cornfields, where black powder had scorched the drying stalks so long ago.

He had brooded many a night over the concept of brother against brother—for real—and wondered what part he might have played if he had been born in time for those terrible and heroic days.

Yet what fascinated him most was that men had given their lives for an idea. Often, when he sat quietly with the woods around him, he dreamed over fighting for something as precious as an idea, and dying proudly.

His mother often told him that a man needed goals, and strong beliefs and pride in the seeking of them. Then she would laugh that deep laugh of hers, tousle his hair and tell him that having pride would never be his problem. He already had too much of it.

He wanted to be the best, the fastest, the strongest, the smartest. It wasn't an easy target, not with three equally determined brothers. So he pushed himself. Studied longer, fought more fiercely, worked harder.

Losing just wasn't an option for Jared MacKade.

"They're coming," Jared whispered.

Devin nodded. He'd been listening to the crackle of twigs, the rustle of brush. Biding his time. "Rafe's that way. Shane circled behind."

Jared didn't question Devin's assessment. His brother had instincts like a cat. "I'll take Rafe. You stay here until we're engaged. Shane'll come running. Then you can take him out."

Anticipation brightened Jared's eyes. The two brothers' hands clutched in a brief salute. "Victory or death."

Jared caught his first sight of the faded blue shirt, a blur of movement as the enemy dashed from tree to tree. With the patience of a snake, he waited, waited. Then, with a blood curdling cry, leaped.

He brought Rafe down in a flying tackle that had them both skittering over the rough dirt into the prickle of wild blackberries.

It was a good surprise attack, but Jared wasn't foolish enough to think that would be the end of it. Rafe was a vicious opponent—as any kid at Antietam Elementary could attest. He fought with a kind of fiendish enjoyment that Jared understood perfectly.

There really was nothing better than pounding someone on a hot summer day when the threat of school was creeping closer and all the morning chores were behind you.

Thorns tore at clothes and scratched flesh. The two boys wrestled back to the path, fists and elbows ramming, sneakers digging in at the heels for purchase. Nearby, a second battle was under way, with curses and grunts and the satisfying crunch of bodies over aged dried leaves.

The MacKade brothers were in heaven.

"You're dead, Rebel scum!" Jared shouted when he managed to grab Rafe in a slippery headlock.

"I'm taking you to hell with me, bluebelly!" Rafe shouted right back.

In the end, they were simply too well matched, and they rolled away from each other, filthy, breathless, and laughing.

Wiping the blood from a split lip, Jared turned his head to watch his troops engage the enemy. It looked to him as though Devin were going to have a black eye, and Shane had a rip in his jeans that was going to get them all in trouble.

He let out a long, contented sigh and watched the sunlight play through the leaves.

"Going to break it up?" Rafe asked, without much interest.

"Nah." Casually, Jared wiped blood from his chin. "They're almost finished."

"I'm going to go into town." Energy still high, Rafe bounded up and brushed off his pants. "Gonna get me a soda down at Ed's."

Devin stopped wrestling Shane and looked over. "Got any money?"

With a wolfish grin, Rafe jingled the change in his pocket. "Maybe." Challenge issued, he tossed the hair out of his eyes, then took off at a dead run.

The delightful prospect of shaking quarters from Rafe's pockets was all the impetus Devin and Shane needed. Suddenly united, they scrambled off each other and chased after him.

"Come on, Jare," Shane called over his shoulder. "We're going to Ed's."

"Go on. I'll catch up."

But he lay there on his back, staring at the sunlight flickering through the awning of leaves. As his brothers' pounding footsteps faded away, he thought he could hear the sounds of the old battle. The boom and crash of mortars, the screams of the dead and dying.

Then, closer, the ragged breathing of the lost and the frightened.

He closed his eyes, too familiar with the ghosts of these woods to be unnerved by their company. He wished he'd known them, could have asked them what it was like to put your life, your soul, at risk. To love a thing, an ideal, a way of life, so much you would give everything you were to defend it.

He thought he would for his family, for his parents, his brothers. But that was different. That was…family.

One day, he promised himself, he would make his mark. People would look at him and know that there was Jared MacKade, a man who stood for something. A man who did what had to be done, and never turned his back on a fight.

Chapter 1

Jared wanted a cold beer. He could already taste it, that first long sip that would start to wash away the dregs of a lousy day in court, an idiot judge and a client who was driving him slowly insane.

He didn't mind that she was guilty as sin, had certainly been an accessory before and after the fact in the spate of petty burglaries in the west end of Hagerstown. He could swallow defending the guilty. That was his job. But he was getting damn sick and tired of having his client hit on him.

The woman had a very skewed view of lawyer-client relations. He could only hope he'd made it clear that if she grabbed his butt again, she was out on hers and on her own.

Under different circumstances, he might have found it only mildly insulting, even fairly amusing. But he had too much on his mind, and on his calendar, to play games.

With an irritated jerk of the wrist, he jammed a classical CD into his car stereo system and let Mozart join him on the winding route toward home.

Just one stop, he told himself. One quick stop, and then a cold beer.

And he wouldn't even have had that one stop, if this Savannah Morningstar had bothered to return his calls.

He rolled his shoulders to ease the tension and punched the gas pedal on a curve to please himself with a bit of illegal speed. He drove along the familiar country road quickly, barely noticing the first tender buds of spring on the trees or the faint haze of wild dogwood ready to bloom.

He braked for a darting rabbit, passed a pickup heading toward Antietam. He hoped Shane had supper started, then remembered with an oath that it was his turn to cook.

The scowl suited his face, with its sculptured lines,

the slight imperfection of a nose that had been broken twice, the hard edge of chin. Behind shaded glasses, under arching black brows, his eyes were cool and sharply green. Though his lips were set in a line of irritation, that didn't detract from the appeal of them.

Women often looked at that mouth, and wondered... When it smiled, and the dimple beside it winked, they sighed and asked themselves how that wife of his had ever let him get away.

He made a commanding presence in a courtroom. The broad shoulders, narrow hips and tough, rangy build always looked polished in a tailored suit, but the elegant cover never quite masked the power beneath.

His black hair had just enough wave to curl appealingly at the collar of one of his starched white shirts.

In the courtroom he wasn't Jared MacKade, one of the MacKade brothers who had run roughshod over the south of the county from the day they were born. He was Jared MacKade, counselor-at-law.

He glanced up at the house on the hill just outside of town. It was the old Barlow place that his brother Rafe had come back to town to buy. He saw Rafe's car at the top of the steep lane, and hesitated.

He was tempted to pull in, to forget about this last

little detail of the day and share that beer he wanted with Rafe. But he knew that if Rafe wasn't working, hammering or sawing, or painting some part of the house that would be a bed and breakfast by fall, he would be waiting for his new wife to come home.

It still amazed Jared that the baddest of the bad MacKades was a married man.

So he drove past, took the left fork in the road that would wind him around toward the MacKade farm and the small plot of land that bordered it.

According to his information, Savannah Morningstar had bought the little house on the edge of the woods only two months before. She lived there with her son and, as the gossip mill was mostly dry where she was concerned, obviously kept to herself.

Jared figured the woman was either stupid or rude. In his experience, when people received a message from a lawyer, they answered it. Though the voice on her answering machine had been low, throaty, and stunningly sexy, he wasn't looking forward to meeting that voice face-to-face. This mission was a favor for a colleague—and a nuisance.

He caught a glimpse of the little house through the trees. More of a cabin, really, he mused, though a second floor had been added several years ago. He turned onto the narrow lane by the Morningstar mailbox, cutting his speed dramatically to negotiate the dips and holes, and studied the house as he approached.

It was log, built originally, as he recalled, as some city doctor's vacation spot. That hadn't lasted long. People from the city often thought they wanted rustic until they had it.

The quiet setting, the trees, the peaceful bubbling of a creek topped off from yesterday's rain, enhanced the ambience of the house, with its simple lines, untreated wood and uncluttered front porch.

The steep bank in front of it was rocky and rough, and in the summer, he knew, tended to be covered with high, tangled weeds. Someone had been at work here, he mused, and almost came to a stop. The earth had been dug and turned, worked to a deep brown. There were still rocks, but they were being used as a natural decorative landscaping. Someone had planted clumps of flowers among them, behind them.

No, he realized, someone *was* planting clumps of flowers. He saw the figure, the movement, as he rounded the crest and brought his car to a halt at the end of the lane, beside an aging compact.

Jared lifted his briefcase, climbed out of the car and started over the freshly mowed swatch of grass. He was very grateful for his dark glasses when Savannah Morningstar rose.

She'd been kneeling amid the dirt and garden tools and flats of flowers. When she moved, she moved slowly, inch by very impressive inch. She was tall—a curvy five-ten, he estimated—filling out a drab yellow T-shirt and ripped jeans to the absolute limit of the law. Her legs were endless.

Her feet were bare and her hands grimed with soil.

The sun glinted on hair as thick and black as his. She wore it down her back in one loose braid. Her eyes were concealed, as his were, behind sunglasses. But what he could see of her face was fascinating.

If a man could get past that truly amazing body, he could spend a lot of time on that face, Jared mused.

Carved cheekbones rose high and taut against skin the color of gold dust. Her mouth was full and un-smiling, her nose straight and sharp, her chin slightly pointed.

"Savannah Morningstar?"

"Yes, that's right."

He recognized the voice from the answering machine. He'd never known a voice and a body that suited each other more perfectly. "I'm Jared MacKade."

She angled her head, and the sun glanced off the amber tint of her glasses. "Well, you look like a lawyer. I haven't done anything—lately—that I need representation for."

"I'm not going door-to-door soliciting clients. I've left several messages on your machine."

"I know." She knelt again to finish planting a hunk of purple phlox. "The handy thing about machines is that you don't have to talk to people you don't want to talk to." Carefully she patted dirt around the shallow roots. "Obviously, I didn't want to talk to you, Lawyer MacKade."

"Not stupid," he declared. "Just rude."

Amused, she tipped her face up to his. "That's right. I am. But since you're here, you might as well tell me what you're so fired up to tell me."

"A colleague of mine in Oklahoma contacted me after he tracked you down."

The quick clutching in Savannah's gut came and went. Deliberately she picked up another clump of phlox. Taking her time, she shifted and hacked at the dirt with her hand spade. "I haven't been in Oklahoma for nearly ten years. I don't remember breaking any laws before I left."

"Your father hired my colleague to locate you."

"I'm not interested." Her flower-planting mood was gone. Because she didn't want to infect the innocent blooms with the poison stirring inside her, she rose again and rubbed her hands on her jeans. "You can tell your colleague to tell my father I'm not interested."

"Your father's dead."

He'd had no intention of telling her that way. He hadn't mentioned her father or his death on the phone, because he didn't have the heart to break such news over a machine. Jared still remembered the swift, searing pain of his own father's death. And his mother's.

She didn't gasp or sway or sob. Standing straight, Savannah absorbed the shock and refused the grief. Once there had been love. Once there had been need. And now, she thought, now there was nothing.

"When?"

"Seven months ago. It took awhile to find you. I'm sorry—"

She interrupted him. "How?"

"A fall. According to my information, he'd been working the rodeo circuit. He took a bad fall, hit his head. He wasn't unconscious long, and refused to go to the hospital for X rays. But he contacted my colleague and gave him instructions. A week later, your father collapsed. An embolism."

She listened without a word, without movement. In her mind Savannah could see the man she'd once known and loved, clinging to the back of a bucking mustang, one hand reaching for the sky.

She could see him laughing, she could see him drunk. She could see him murmuring endearments to an aging mare, and she could see him burning with rage and shame as he turned his own daughter, his only child, away.

But she couldn't see him dead.

"Well, you've told me." With that, she turned toward the house.

"Ms. Morningstar." If he had heard grief in her voice, he would have given her privacy. But there'd been nothing at all in her voice.

"I'm thirsty." She headed up the walkway that cut through the grass, then climbed onto the porch and let the screen door slam behind her.

Yeah? Jared thought, fuming. Well, so was he. And he was damn well going to finish up this business and get a cold one himself. He walked into the house without bothering to knock.

The small living room held furniture built for comfort, chairs with deep, sagging cushions, sturdy tables that would bear the weight of resting feet. The walls were a shade of umber that melded nicely with the pine of the floor. There were vivid splashes of color to offset and challenge the mellow tones—paintings, pillows, a scatter of toys over bright rugs that reminded him she had a child.

He stepped through into a kitchen with brilliantly white counters and the same gleaming pine floor, where she stood in front of the sink, scrubbing garden earth from her hands. She didn't bother to speak, but dried them off before she took a pitcher of lemonade from the refrigerator.

"I'd like to get this over with as much as you," he told her.

She let out a breath, took her sunglasses off and tossed them on the counter. Wasn't his fault, she reminded herself. Not completely, anyway. When you came down to it, and added all the pieces together, there was no one to blame.

"You look hot." She poured lemonade into a tall

glass, handed it to him. After giving him one quick glimpse of almond-shaped eyes the color of melted chocolate, she turned away to get another glass.

"Thanks."

"Are you going to tell me he had debts that I'm obliged to settle? If you are, I'm going to tell you I have no intention of doing so." The jittering in her stomach had nearly calmed, so she leaned back against the counter and crossed her bare feet at the ankles. "I've made what I've got, and I intend to keep it."

"Your father left you seven thousand, eight hundred and twenty-five dollars. And some change."

He watched the glass stop, hesitate, then continue to journey to her lips. She drank slowly, thoughtfully. "Where did he get seven thousand dollars?"

"I have no idea. But the money is currently in a passbook savings account in Tulsa." Jared set his briefcase down on the small butcher-block table, opened it. "You have only to show me proof of identity and sign these papers, and your inheritance will be transferred to you."

"I don't want it." Her first sign of emotion was the crack of glass against counter. "I don't want his money."

Jared set the papers on the table. "It's your money."

"I said I don't want it."

Patiently Jared slipped off his own glasses and hooked them in his top pocket. "I understand you were estranged from your father."

"You don't understand anything," she shot back. "All you need to know is that I don't want the damn money. So put your papers back in your fancy briefcase and get out."

Well used to arguments, Jared kept his eyes—and his temper—level. "Your father's instructions were that if you were unwilling or unable to claim the inheritance, it was to go to your child."

Her eyes went molten. "Leave my son out of this."

"The legalities—"

"Hang your legalities. He's my son. Mine. And it's my choice. We don't want or need the money."

"Ms. Morningstar, you can refuse the terms of your father's will, which means the courts will get involved and complicate what should be a very simple, straightforward matter. Hell, do yourself a favor. Take it, blow it on a weekend in Reno, give it to charity, bury it in a tin can in the yard."

She forced herself to calm down, not an easy matter when her emotions were up. "It is very simple and straightforward. I'm not taking his money." Her head jerked around at the sound of the front door slamming. "My son," she said, and shot Jared a lethal look. "Don't you say anything to him about this."

"Hey, Mom! Connor and me—" He skidded to a halt, a tall, skinny boy with his mother's eyes and messy black hair crushed under a backward fielder's cap. He studied Jared with a mix of distrust and curiosity. "Who's he?"

Manners ran in the family, Jared decided. Lousy ones. "I'm Jared MacKade, a neighbor."

"You're Shane's brother." The boy walked over, picked up his mother's lemonade and drank it down in several noisy gulps. "He's cool. That's where we were, me and Connor," he told his mother. "Over at the MacKade farm. This big orange cat had kittens."

"Again?" Jared muttered. "This time I'm taking her to the vet personally and having her spayed. You were with Connor," Jared added. "Connor Dolin."

"Yeah." Suspicious, the boy watched him over the rim of his glass.

"His mother's a friend of mine," Jared said simply.

Savannah's hand rested briefly, comfortably, on her son's shoulder. "Bryan, go upstairs and scrape some of the dirt off. I'm going to start dinner."

"Okay."

"Nice to have met you, Bryan."

The boy looked surprised, then flashed a quick grin. "Yeah, cool. See you."

"He looks like you," Jared commented.

"Yes, he does." Her mouth softened slightly at the sound of feet clumping up the stairs. "I'm thinking about putting in soundproofing."

"I'm trying to get a picture of him palling around with Connor."

The amusement in her eyes fired into temper so quickly it fascinated him. "And you have a problem with that?"

"I'm trying to get a picture," Jared repeated, "of the live wire that just headed upstairs and the quiet, painfully shy Connor Dolin. Kids as confident as your son don't usually choose boys like Connor for friends."

Temper smoothed out. "They just clicked. Bryan hasn't had a lot of opportunity to keep friends. We've moved around a great deal. That's changing."

"What brought you here?"

"I was—" She broke off, and her lips curved. "Now you're trying to be neighborly so that I'll soften up and take this little problem off your hands. Forget it."

She turned to take a package of chicken breasts out of the refrigerator.

"Seven thousand dollars is a lot of money. If you put it in a college fund now, it would give your son a good start when he's ready for it."

"When and if Bryan's ready for college, I'll put him through myself."

"I understand about pride, Ms. Morningstar. That's why it's easy for me to see when it's misplaced."

She turned again and flipped her braid behind her shoulder. "You must be the patient, by-the-book, polite type, Mr. MacKade."

The grin that beamed out at her nearly made her blink. She was sure there were states where that kind of weapon was illegal.

"Don't get to town much, do you?" Jared murmured. "You'd hear different. Ask Connor's mama about the MacKades sometime, Ms. Morningstar. I'll leave the papers." He slipped his sunglasses on again. "You think it over and get back to me. I'm in the book."

She stayed where she was, a frown on her face and a cold package of raw chicken in her hands. She was still there when his car's engine roared to life and her son came darting back down the stairs.

Quickly she snatched up the papers and pushed them into the closest drawer.

"What was he here for?" Bryan wanted to know. "How come he was wearing a suit?"

"A lot of men wear suits." She would evade, but she wouldn't lie, not to Bryan. "And stay out of the refrigerator. I'm starting dinner."

With his hand on the door of the fridge, Bryan rolled his eyes. "I'm starving. I can't wait for dinner."

Savannah plucked an apple from a bowl and tossed it over her shoulder, smiling to herself when she heard the solid smack of Bryan's catch.

"Shane said it was okay if we went by after school tomorrow and looked at the kittens some more. The farm's really cool, Mom. You should see."

"I've seen farms before."

"Yeah, but this one's neat. He's got two dogs. Fred and Ethel."

"Fred and—" She broke off into laughter. "Maybe I will have to see that."

"And from the hayloft you can see clear into town. Connor says part of the battle was fought right there on the fields. Probably dead guys everywhere."

"Now that sounds really enticing."

"And I was thinking—" Bryan crunched into his apple, tried to sound casual "—you'd maybe want to come over and look at the kittens."

"Oh, would I?"

"Well, yeah. Connor said maybe Shane would give some away when they were weaned. You might want one."

She set a lid on the chicken she was sautéing. "I would?"

"Sure, yeah, for, like, company when I'm in school." He smiled winningly. "So you wouldn't get lonely."

Savannah shifted her weight onto her hip and studied him owlishly. "That's a good one, Bry. Really smooth."

That was what he'd been counting on. "So can I?"

She would have given him the world, not just one small kitten. "Sure." Her laughter rolled free when he launched himself into her arms.

With the meal over, the dishes done, the homework that terrified her finished and the child who was her life tucked into bed with his ball cap, Savannah sat on the front-porch swing and watched the woods.

She enjoyed the way night always deepened there first, as if it had a primary claim. Later there might be the hoot of an owl, or the rumbling low of Shane MacKade's cattle. Sometimes, if it was very quiet, or there'd been rain, she could hear the bubble of creek over rocks.

It was too early in the spring yet for the flash and shimmer of fireflies. She looked forward to them, and hoped Bryan wasn't yet beyond the stage where he would chase them. She wanted to watch him run in his own yard in the starlight on a warm summer night when the flowers were blooming, the air was thick with their perfume, and the woods were a dense curtain closing them off from everyone and everything.

She wanted him to have a kitten to play with, friends to call his own, a childhood filled with moments that lasted forever.

A childhood that would be everything hers had never been.

Setting the swing into motion, she leaned back and drank in the absolute quiet of a country night.

It had taken her ten long, hard years to get here, on this swing, on this porch, in this house. There wasn't a moment of it she regretted. Not the sacrifice, the pain, the worry, the risk. Because to regret one was to regret all. To regret one was to regret Bryan. And that was impossible.

She had exactly what she had strived for now, and

she had earned it herself, despite odds brutally stacked against her.

She was exactly where she wanted to be, who she wanted to be, and no ghost from the past would spoil it for her.

How dare he offer her money, when all she'd ever wanted was his love?

So Jim Morningstar was dead. The hard-drinking, hard-living, hardheaded son of a bitch had ridden his last bronco, roped his last bull. Now she was supposed to grieve. Now she was supposed to be grateful that, at the end, he'd thought of her. He'd thought of the grandchild he'd never wanted, never even seen.

He'd chosen his pride over his daughter, and the tiny flicker of life that had been inside her. Now, after all this time, he'd thought to make up for that with just under eight thousand dollars.

The hell with him, Savannah thought wearily, and closed her eyes. Eight million couldn't make her forget, and it sure as hell couldn't buy her forgiveness. And no lawyer in a fancy suit with killer eyes and a silver tongue was going to change her mind.

Jared MacKade could go to hell right along with Jim Morningstar.

He'd had no business coming onto her land as if he

belonged there, standing in her kitchen sipping lemonade, talking about college funds, smiling so sweetly at her boy. He'd had no right to aim that smile at her—not so outrageously—and stir up all those juices that she'd deliberately let go flat and dry.

Well, she wasn't dead, after all, she thought with a heartfelt sigh. Some men seemed to have been created to stir a woman's juices.

She didn't want to sit here on this beautiful spring night and think about how long it had been since she'd held a man, or been held. She really didn't want to think at all, but he'd walked across her lawn and shaken her laboriously constructed world in less time than it took to blink.

Her father was dead, and she was very much alive. Lawyer MacKade had made those two facts perfectly clear in one short visit.

However much she wanted to avoid it, she was going to have to deal with both those facts. Eventually she would have to face Jared again. If she didn't seek him out, she was certain, he'd be back. He had that bull dog look about him, pretty suit and tie or not.

So, she would have to decide what to do. And she would have to tell Bryan. He had a right to know his grandfather was dead. He had a right to know about the legacy.

But just for tonight, she wouldn't think, she wouldn't worry, she wouldn't wonder.

She wasn't aware for a long time that her cheeks were wet, her shoulders were shaking, the sobs were tearing at her throat. Curling into a ball, she buried her face against her knees.

"Oh, Daddy…"

Chapter 2

Jared wasn't opposed to farm work. He wouldn't care to make it a living, as Shane did, but he wasn't opposed to putting in a few hours now and again. Since he'd put his house in town on the market and moved back home, he pitched in whenever he had the time. It was the kind of work you never forgot, the rhythms easy to fall back into—ones your muscles soon remembered. The milking, the feeding, the plowing, the sowing.

Stripped down to a sweaty T-shirt and old jeans, he hauled out hay bales for the dairy stock. The black-and-white cows lumbered for the trough, wide, sturdy bodies bumping, tails swishing. The scent of them was a reminder of youth, of his father most of all.

Buck MacKade had tended his cows well, and had taught his boys to see them as a responsibility, as well as a way of making a living. For him, the farm had been very simply a way of life—and Jared knew the same was true of Shane. He wondered now, as he fell back into the routine of tending, what his father would have thought of his oldest son, the lawyer.

He probably would have been a little baffled by the choice of suit and tie, of paper drafted and filed, of appearances and appointments. But Jared hoped he would have been proud. He needed to believe his father would have been proud.

But this wasn't such a bad way to spend a Saturday, he mused, after a week of courtrooms and paperwork.

Nearby, Shane whistled a mindless tune and herded the cows in to feed. And looked, Jared realized, very much as their father would have—dusty jeans, dusty shirt loose on a tough, disciplined body, worn cap over hair that needed a barber's touch.

"What do you think of the new neighbor?" Jared called out.

"Huh?"

"The new neighbor," Jared repeated, and jerked a thumb in the direction of Morningstar land.

"Oh, you mean the goddess." Shane stepped away from the trough, eyes dreamy. "I need a moment of silence," he murmured, and crossed his hands over his heart.

Amused, Jared swiped a hand through his hair. "She is impressive."

"She's built like… I don't have words." Shane gave one of the cows an affectionate slap on the rump. "I've only seen her once. Ran into her and her kid going into the market. Talked to her for about two minutes, drooled for the next hour."

"How did she strike you?"

"Like a bolt of lightning, bro."

"Think you can keep your head out of your shorts for a minute?"

"I can try." Shane bent to help break up bales. "Like a woman who can handle herself and isn't looking for company," he decided. "Good with the kid. You can tell just by the way they stand together."

"Yeah, I noticed that."

Shane's interest was piqued. "When?"

"I was over there a couple of days ago. Had a little legal business."

"Oh." Shane wiggled his eyebrows. "Privileged communication?"

"That's right." Jared hauled over another bale and nipped the twine. "What's the word on her?"

"There isn't much of anything. From what I get, she was in the Frederick area, saw the ad for the cabin in the paper down there. Then she blew into town, snapped up the property, put her kid in school and closed herself off on her little hill. It's driving Mrs. Metz crazy."

"I bet. If Mrs. Metz, queen of the grapevine, can't get any gossip on her, nobody can."

"If you're handling some legal deal for her, you ought to be able to shake something loose."

"She's not a client," Jared said, and left it at that. "The boy comes around here?"

"Now and again. He and Connor."

"An odd pairing."

"It's nice seeing them together. Bry's a pistol, let me tell you. He's got a million questions, opinions, arguments." Shane lifted a brow. "Reminds me of somebody."

"That so?"

"Dad always said if there were two opinions on one subject, you'd have both of them. The kid's like that. And he makes Connor laugh. It's good to hear."

"The boy hasn't had enough to laugh about, not with a father like Joe Dolin."

Shane grunted, gathering up discarded twine. "Well, Dolin's behind bars and out of the picture." Shane stepped back, checking over his herd and the land beyond. "He's not going to be beating up on Cassie anymore, or terrorizing those kids. The divorce going to be final soon?"

"We should have a final decree within sixty days."

"Can't be soon enough. I have to see to the hogs. You want to get another bale out of the barn?"

"Sure."

Shane headed over to the pen, prepared to mix feed. At the sight of him, the fat pigs began to stir and snort. "Yeah, Daddy's here, boys and girls."

"He talks to them all the time," Bryan announced from behind them.

"They talk right back." With a grin, Shane turned, and saw that the boy wasn't alone.

Savannah stood with one hand on her son's shoulder and an easy smile. Her hair was loose, falling like black rain over the shoulders of a battered denim jacket. Shane decided the pigs could wait, and leaned on the fence.

"Good morning."

"Good morning." She stepped forward, looked into the pen. "They look hungry."

"They're always hungry. That's why we call them pigs."

She laughed and propped a foot on the bottom rung of the fence. She was a woman used to the sight, sound and smell of animals. "That one there certainly looks well fed."

He shifted closer so he could enjoy the scent of her hair. "She's full of piglets. I'll have to separate her soon."

"Spring on the farm," she murmured. "So, who's the daddy?"

"That smug-looking hog over there."

"Ah, the one who's ignoring her. Typical." Still smiling, she tossed back her hair. "We're here on a mission, Mr. MacKade."

"Shane."

"Shane. Rumor is, you've got kittens."

Shane grinned down at Bryan. "Talked her into it, huh?"

All innocence, Bryan shrugged, but his quick, triumphant grin betrayed him. "She needs company when I'm at school."

"That's a good one. They're in the barn. I'll show you."

"No." To stop him, Savannah put a hand on his arm. There was a glint in her eyes that told him she knew exactly where his thoughts were heading. "We won't interrupt your work. Your pigs are waiting, and I'm sure Bryan knows exactly where to find the kittens."

"Sure I do. Come on, Mom." He had her by the hand, tugging. "They're really cool. Shane's got all kinds of neat animals," Bryan told her.

"Mm-hmm..." With a last amused glance, she let herself be hauled away. "Magnificent animals." And, she thought as she watched Jared stride out of the barn with a bale over his shoulder, here was another one now.

His eyes met hers, held, as he stopped, tossed the bale down. The suit had been deceiving, she realized. Though he hadn't looked soft in it, he'd looked elegant. There was nothing elegant about the man now.

He was all muscle.

If she'd been a lesser woman, her mouth might have watered.

Instead, she inclined her head and spoke coolly. "Mr. MacKade."

"Ms. Morningstar." His tone was just as cool. But it took a focused effort to unknot the tension in his stomach. "Hi, Bryan."

"I didn't know you worked here," Bryan began. "I've never seen you working here."

"Now and again."

"How come you were wearing a suit?" he asked. "Shane never wears a suit."

"Not unless you knock him unconscious first." When the boy grinned, Jared noticed a gap in his teeth that hadn't been there the day before. "Lose something?"

Proudly Bryan pressed his tongue in the gap. "It came out this morning. It's good for spitting."

"I used to hold the record around here. Nine feet, three inches. Without the wind."

Impressed, and challenged, Bryan worked up saliva in his mouth, concentrated and let it fly. Jared pursed his lips, nodded. "Not bad."

"I can do better than that."

"You're one of the tops in your division, Bry," Savannah said dryly. "But Mr. MacKade has work to do, and we're supposed to be looking at kittens."

"Yeah, they're right in here." He took off into the barn at a run. Savannah followed more slowly.

"Nine feet?" she murmured, with a glance over her shoulder.

"And three inches."

"You surprise me, Mr. MacKade."

She had a way of sauntering on those long legs, he thought, that gave a man's eyes a mind of their own. After a quick internal debate, he gave up and went in after her.

"Aren't they great?" Bryan plopped right down in the hay beside the litter of sleeping kittens and their very bored-looking mama. "They have to stay with her for weeks and weeks." Very gently, he stroked a fingertip over the downy head of a smoke-gray kitten. "But then we can take one."

She couldn't help it. Savannah went soft all over. "Oh, they're so tiny." Crouching down, she gave in to the need and lifted one carefully into her hand. "Look, Bry, it fits right in my palm. Oh, aren't you sweet?" Murmuring, she nuzzled her face against the fur. "Aren't you pretty?"

"I like this one best." Bryan continued to stroke the tiny gray bundle. "I'm going to call him Cal. Like for Cal Ripkin."

"Oh." The soft orange ball in her hand stirred and mewed thinly. Her heart was lost. "All right. The gray one."

"You could take two." Jared stepped into the stall. Her face, he thought, was an open book. "It's nice for them to have company."

"Two?" The idea burst like a thousand watts in Bryan's brain. "Yeah, Mom, we'll take two. One would be lonely!"

"Bry—"

"And it wouldn't be any more trouble. We've got lots of room now. Cal's going to want somebody to play with, to hang around with."

"Thanks, MacKade."

"My pleasure."

"And anyway," Bryan went on, because he'd come out of his own excitement long enough to see the way his mother was cuddling the orange kitten, "this way we could each pick one. That's the fair way, right?"

Smiling, Bryan reached out to brush his finger over

the orange kitten. "He likes you. See, he's trying to lick your hand."

"He's hungry," Savannah told him, but she knew there was no possible way she was going to be able to resist the little bundle rooting in her hand. "I suppose they would be company for each other."

"All right, Mom!" Bryan sprang up, kissed her without any of the embarrassment many nine-year-old boys might feel. "I'm going to tell Shane which ones are ours."

With a clatter of feet, Bryan dashed out of the barn.

"You know you wanted it," Jared said.

"I'm old enough to know I can't have everything I want." But she sighed and set the kitten down so that it could join its siblings in a morning snack. "But two cats can't be that much more trouble than one."

She started to rise, flicking a glance upward when Jared put a hand under her arm and helped her up. "Thanks." She stepped around him and headed for the light. "So, are you a farm boy moonlighting as a lawyer, or a lawyer moonlighting as a farm boy?"

"It feels like both these days. I spent the last few years living in Hagerstown." He matched his pace to her long, lazy one. "When I moved back a couple of months ago, I had a lot of things to deal with in the city, so I haven't been able to give Shane and Devin much of a hand."

"Devin?" She paused outside, where the sun was strong and warming quickly. "Oh, the sheriff. Yes, Bryan's mentioned him. He lives here, too."

"He sleeps here now and again," Jared said. "He lives in the sheriff's office."

"Fighting crime, in a town with two stoplights?"

"Devin takes things seriously." He looked over to where Bryan was dancing around Shane as Shane herded the cows back to pasture. "Have you given any more thought to your father's estate?"

"*Estate*. Now, that's a very serious word. Yes, I've thought about it. I have to talk to Bryan." At Jared's cocked brow, she spoke quietly. "We're a team, Mr. MacKade. He gets a vote in this. We have a Little League game this afternoon, and I don't want to distract him from that. I'll have an answer for you by Monday."

"Fine." Jared's eyes shifted from hers again, narrowed. The warning glint in them had Savannah's lips curving.

"Let me guess. Your brother's looking at my butt again."

Intrigued, Jared looked back at her. "You can tell?"

Her laugh was quick and rich. "Honey, women can always tell. Sometimes we let you get away with it, that's all." She cast a lightning grin over her shoulder, winked at Shane. "Come on, Bryan. You've got chores to finish up before the game."

She walked back through the woods with Bryan, listening to him chatter endlessly about the kittens, the ball game, the animals at the MacKade farm.

He was happy, was all she could think. He was safe. She'd done a good job. On her own. She caught herself before she could sigh and alert her son to the troubles in her mind. It was often so hard to know what was right.

"Why don't you run ahead, Bry? Get those chores done and change into your uniform. I think I'll sit here awhile."

He stopped, kicked at a pebble. "How come you sit here so much?"

"Because I like it here."

He studied her face, looked for signs. "We're really going to stay in this place?"

Her heart broke a little as she bent down and kissed him. "Yes, we're really going to stay."

His grin was quick and bright. "Cool."

He raced off, leaving her standing alone in the path.

She sat on a fallen log, closed her eyes and emptied her mind.

So much tried to intrude—memories, mistakes, doubts. She willed them away, concentrating on the quiet and that place in her own head that was safe from worry.

It was a trick she'd learned as a child, when the confusion of life had been too overwhelming to face. There had been long rides in a rattling pickup, endless hours in smelly paddocks, loud voices, the gnaw of real hunger, the cries of fretful babies, the chill of underheated rooms. They could all be faced, again and again, if she could just escape into herself for a few minutes.

Decisions became clearer, confidence could be rebuilt.

As fascinated as if he'd come across some mythical creature in the woods, Jared watched her. That exotic face was utterly peaceful, her body utterly still. He wouldn't have been surprised to see a butterfly or a bright bird land on her shoulder.

These woods had always been his. His personal place. His intimate place. Yet seeing her here didn't feel like an intrusion. It seemed expected, as if in some part of his mind he'd known he'd find her here if he just knew when to look.

He realized he was afraid to blink, as if in that fraction of a second she might vanish, never to be found again.

She opened her eyes slowly and looked directly into his.

For a moment, neither of them could speak. Savannah felt the breath rush into her throat and stick there. She was used to men staring at her. They had done so even when she was a child. It annoyed, amused or interested her by turns. But it had never left her speechless, as this one long, unblinking stare out of eyes the color of summer grass did.

He moved first, stepping closer. And the world started again.

"I hate stating the obvious." Because he wanted to— and because his knees were just a little weak—he sat on the log beside her. "But you are staggering."

Steadier now, she inclined her head. "Aren't you supposed to be plowing a field or something?"

"Shane's gotten proprietary about his tractor over the years. Aren't you supposed to be going to a ball game?"

"It's not for a couple hours." Savannah took a deep

breath, relieved that it went smoothly in and out. "So, who's trespassing, you or me?"

"Technically, both of us." Jared took out a slim cigar and found a match. "This is my brother's property."

"I assumed the farm belonged to all of you."

"It does." He took a drag, watched the smoke drift into the sunlight. "This strip here is Rafe's land."

"Rafe?" Her brows shot up. "Don't tell me there are more of you."

"Four altogether." He tried to smother his surprise when she plucked the cigar out of his fingers and helped herself to a casual drag.

"Four MacKades," she mused. "It's a wonder the town survived. And none of the women managed to rope you in?"

"Rafe's married. I was."

"Oh." She handed him back the cigar. "And now you're back on the farm."

"That right. Actually, if I hadn't waffled, I'd be living in your cabin."

"Is that so?"

"Yep. My place in town's on the market and I'm looking for something around here. But you already had a contract on your place by the time I started looking."

He picked up a stick and drew in the dirt. "The farm," he said, sketching lines. "Rafe's. The cabin."

Savannah pursed her lips at the triangle. "Hmm... And the MacKades would have owned a nice chunk of the mountain. You missed your shot, Lawyer MacKade."

"So it seems, Ms. Morningstar."

"I suppose you can call me Savannah, since we're neighbors." Taking the stick from him, she tapped the point of the triangle. "This place. It's the stone house you can see on the hill from the road into town?"

"That's right. The old Barlow place."

"It's haunted."

"You've heard the stories?"

"No." Interested, she looked over at him. "Are there stories?"

It only took him a moment to see she wasn't playing games. "Why did you say it was haunted?"

"You can feel it," she said simply. "Just like these woods. They're restless." When he continued to stare at her, she smiled. "Indian blood. I'm part Apache. My father liked to claim he was full-blooded, but..." She let words trail off, looked away.

"But?"

"There's Italian, Mexican, even a little French mixed in."

"Your mother?"

"Anglo and Mex. She was a barrel racer. Rodeo champion. She was in a car accident when I was five. I don't remember her very clearly."

"Both of mine are gone, too." Companionably he offered her the cigar. "It's tough."

She drew in smoke. "This one shouldn't have been, for me. I lost my father ten years ago, when he booted me out. I was sixteen, and pregnant with Bryan."

"I'm sorry, Savannah."

"Hey, I got by." She passed back the cigar. She didn't know why she'd told him, except that it was quiet here, and he listened well. "The thing is, Jared, I've been thinking more about my father in the last day or so than I have in years. You can't imagine what eight thousand dollars would have meant to me ten years ago. Five." With a shrug, she pushed back her hair. "Hell, there was a time eight dollars would have made the difference between— Well, it doesn't matter."

Without thinking, he laid a hand over hers. "Sure it does."

She frowned down at their hands, then slowly, casually, slipped hers away and stood. "The thing is, I have Bryan to think of. So I'll talk this over with him."

"Let me state the obvious again. You've done a terrific job raising your son."

She smiled. "We've raised each other. But thanks. I'll be in touch."

"Savannah." He rose, faced her on the path. "This is a good town, mostly a kind one. No one has to be alone here unless they want to."

"That's something else I have to think about. I'll see you around, Lawyer MacKade."

Jared hadn't been to a Little League game in years. When he pulled up at the park just outside of town and absorbed the scents and sounds, he wondered why. The single swatch of wooden stands was crowded and noisy. And kids who weren't on the field were running and racing behind the low chain-link fence or wrestling under the shade of the stands.

The concession stand drew others, with the smell of steaming hot dogs and sloppy joes.

He pulled his car behind the long line of others along the bumpy shoulder of the narrow road and walked across the uneven grass. He had an eye peeled for

Savannah, but it was little Connor Dolin who caught his gaze.

The pale-haired boy was waiting quietly in line for food, staring at his feet as a couple of burly older kids harassed him.

"Hey, it's nerd brain Dolin. How's your old man like his cell?"

Connor stood stoically as they bumped and shoved him. The woman ahead of him in line turned and clucked her tongue at them, which had no effect at all.

"Why don't you bake him a cake with a file in it, butthead? Bet a wussy like you bakes a real good cake."

"Hey, Connor." Jared stepped up, aimed one look that had the two bullies scrambling away. "How's it going?"

"Okay." Humiliation had stained his cheeks, fear of abuse had dampened his palms around the money he clutched. "I'm supposed to get hot dogs and stuff."

"Mm-hmm." In the way of males, Jared knew better than to mention what he'd just seen. "How come you're not playing ball?"

"I'm not any good." It was said matter-of-factly. He was much too used to being told he wasn't any good to question it. "But Bryan's playing. Bryan Morningstar. He's the best on the team."

"Is he?" Touched by the sudden light in those shy gray eyes, Jared reached out to flip up the visor of Connor's ball cap. The boy jerked instinctively, went still, and reminded Jared that life had not been all ball games and hot dogs for this nine-year-old. "I'm looking forward to watching him," Jared continued, as if the moment had never happened. "What position does he play?"

Ashamed of his own cowardice, Connor studied the ground again. "Shortstop."

"Yeah? I used to play short."

"You did?" Astonished by the idea, Connor just stared.

"That's right. Devin played third, and—"

"Sheriff MacKade played baseball?" Now the astonishment was mixed with a pure case of hero worship. "I bet he was real good."

"He was okay." It pricked the pride, just a little, to remember he'd never been able to outhit, or outfield Devin. "How many dogs you want, Connor?"

"I've got money. Mom gave me money. And Ms. Morningstar." He fumbled with the bills. "I'm supposed to get one for her, too. With mustard."

"It's my treat." Jared held up three fingers at the

vendor as Bryan worried his lip and stared at his money. "This way I get to hang out with you and Ms. Morningstar."

Jared handed the boy the first hot dog, watched him carefully, deliberately squeeze on a line of bright yellow mustard. "Are your mother and sister here?"

"No, sir. Mom's working, and Emma's with her down at the diner. She said it was okay for me to come down and watch, though."

Jared added drinks to the order, and packed the whole business up in a flimsy cardboard box. "Can you handle this?"

"Yes, sir. Sure." Pleased to have been given the job, Connor walked toward the stands, holding the box as if the hot dogs were explosives and the soft drinks a lit match. "We're way up at the top, 'cause Ms. Morningstar says you can see everything better from up high."

And he could see her, Jared mused, as they approached the stands. She sat with her elbows on her knees, her chin cupped in her hands. And her eyes— though he had to imagine, as they were shielded with dark glasses—focused on the field.

He was wrong about that. She was watching him, walking beside the boy, flashing that killer smile or giving a quick salute whenever someone hailed him. And noticing several women—of varying ages—who put their shoulders back or patted at their hair as he passed.

That was what a man who looked like that did to a woman, Savannah supposed. Made her instinctively aware of herself on a purely physical level. It was like pheromones, she decided. The scent of sex.

Those long legs of his carried him up the stands behind the small boy. Now and again his hand touched a shoulder or shook a hand. Savannah picked up the jacket she'd set in Connor's place and squeezed over toward the rail.

"Nice day for a ball game," Jared said as he sat beside her. He took the box from Connor and, to make room for the boy, shifted closer to the woman. "Crowded."

"It is now. Thanks, Con."

"Mr. MacKade bought them," Connor told her, and solemnly handed her back her money.

She started to tell him to keep it, but she understood pride. "Thanks, Mr. MacKade."

"What's the score?"

"We're down one, bottom of the third." She took a healthy bite of her hot dog. "But the top of our batting order's coming up."

"Bryan bats third." Connor chewed and swallowed politely before he spoke. "He has the most RBIs."

Jared watched the first boy come out in the bright orange uniform of the team sponsored by Ed's Café. "Have you met Edwina Crump?" Jared murmured near Savannah's ear.

"Not yet. She owns the diner where Cassandra works, doesn't she?"

"Yeah. Be grateful your boy's not wearing lipstick pink."

Savannah started to comment, then let out an encouraging shout when the bat cracked. The crowd hollered with her when the batter raced to first.

"Tying run's on, right, Con?"

"Yes'm. That's J. D. Bristol. He's a good runner."

She devoured her hot dog, fueling her nerves, while the second batter struck out, swinging. Someone shouted abuse at the ump, and several hot debates erupted in the stands.

"Apparently these games are taken as seriously as ever," Jared commented.

"Baseball's a serious business," Savannah muttered. Her stomach did a fast boogie as Bryan stepped toward the plate.

Now the crowd murmured.

"That's the Morningstar kid," someone announced. "Got a hot bat."

"Way that pitcher's hurling, he's going to need a torch. Nobody's getting a good piece of that ball today."

Savannah lifted her chin, and bumped the man in front of her with her knee. "You just watch," she told him when he glanced around. "He'll get all of it."

Jared grinned and leaned back on the iron rail. "Yeah, a serious business."

She winced when Bryan took a hard swing and met air. "I've got a buck says he knocks the tying run in."

"I don't like to bet against your boy, or the home team," Jared mused. "But MacKades are betting men. A buck it is."

Savannah held her breath as Bryan went through his little batter's routine. Out of the box, kicking at dirt with his left foot, then his right, adjusting his helmet, taking two practice swings.

"Eye on the ball, Bry," she murmured when he stepped to the plate. "Keep your eye on the ball."

He did—as it sailed past him and into the catcher's mitt.

"Strike two."

"What the hell kind of call is that?" she demanded. "That was low and outside. Anybody could see that was low and outside."

The man in front of her turned around, nodded seriously. "It surely was. Bo Perkins's got eyes like my grandma, and she needs glasses to see her own opinion."

"Well, somebody ought to give Bo Perkins a kick in the..." She let the words trail off, remembering Connor who was watching her with huge eyes. "Strike zone," she decided.

"Good save," Jared said under his breath, and watched Bryan step to the plate again.

The pitcher wound up, delivered. And Bryan gave a mighty swing that caught the ball on the meat of the bat. It flew above the leaping gloves of the infield, and rose beautifully over the outfield grass.

"It's gone!" Savannah shouted, leaping to her feet with the rest of the crowd. "That's the way, Bry!" Her victory dance wiggled her hips in a way that distracted Jared from watching the running of the bases. She kept shouting, her hands cupped to carry the sound, while Bryan rounded the bases and stomped on home plate.

For the hell of it, she grabbed her new friend in front

of her and kissed him full on his mouth. "He got a piece of it, didn't he?"

The man, thirty years her senior, blushed like a schoolboy. "Yes, ma'am, he sure did."

"Not exactly the shy, retiring type, are you?" Jared said when she dropped back onto her seat.

"Pay up." She stuck out her hand, palm up.

Jared took out a bill, held it out. "It was worth it."

"You ain't seen nothing yet, Lawyer MacKade."

Jared thought about the promise of those agile, curvy hips and sincerely hoped not.

Chapter 3

It was probably a mistake, Savannah thought, to be sitting across a booth at Ed's from Jared MacKade, eating ice cream. But he'd been very persuasive. And Bryan and Connor had been so excited when he offered to treat them to a victory sundae after the Antietam Cannons batted their way to a win.

And it did give her a chance to see him with Cassandra Dolin.

Connor's mother was a frail little thing, Savannah mused. Blonde and pretty as a china doll, with eyes so haunted they could break your heart. Jared was very gentle with her, very sweet, coaxing smiles from her.

Evidently the shy, vulnerable type was right up his alley.

"Come on, Cassie, have some ice cream with us."

"I can't." Cassie paused by their table long enough to brush a hand over her daughter's hair as little Emma ate her hot fudge with tiny, serious bites. "We're swamped. But I appreciate you treating the kids, Jared."

She was thin enough to blow away in a spring breeze, Jared thought, and held up a spoonful of sundae. "Have a bite, anyway."

She flushed, but opened her mouth as obediently as a child when he held the spoon to her lips. "It's wonderful."

"Hey, Cass, burgers up."

"Right there." Cassie hurried off to pick up the orders from the counter where Edwina Crump reigned supreme.

The owner of the diner sent Jared a lusty wink. The fact that she was twenty years his senior didn't stop her from appreciating a fine-looking man. "Hey, big fellow, don't see you in here often enough." She patted her frizzed red bowling ball of a hairdo. "When you taking me dancing?"

"Whenever you say, Ed."

She gave a chicken-cackle laugh, wiggled her bony body. "Got a hot band over at the Legion tonight. I'm ready and waiting," she told him before she swung back into the kitchen.

Amused, Savannah propped her elbows on the table. "The Legion, huh? I bet it gets pretty wild."

"You'd be surprised." He cocked a brow. "Wanna go?"

"I'll pass, thanks. Bry, do you think you can shovel any more into your mouth at one time?"

He scooped up a dripping spoon of ice cream, butterscotch and sprinkles. "It's great," he said around it. "What's yours taste like, Con?" To see for himself, Bryan reached over the table to dip his spoon into Connor's. "Strawberry's okay," he decided, "but butterscotch is the best."

Willing to be wrong, he eyed Emma's hot fudge avariciously.

"No," Savannah said mildly, and watched with approval as the five-year-old Emma curled a hand protectively around her bowl. She might be a quiet one, Savannah mused, but the kid knew what was hers. "Pack it away, honey," Savannah told her. "I bet you can eat these boys under the table."

"I like ice cream," Emma said, with one of her rare smiles.

"Me too." With a grin, Savannah scooped up some of her own. "And hot fudge is the best, right?"

"Uh-huh, and the whipped cream. Miss Ed gives you lots of it." She put her spoon down carefully beside her empty bowl and announced, "I can go to Regan's now. My mama said."

"What's Regan's?" Bryan wanted to know.

"She's friends with my mom," Connor told him. "She has a shop just down the street. It has lots of neat things to look at."

"Let's go see."

Before he could dart from the booth, Savannah laid a hand on his arm. "Bryan."

It took him a minute. "Oh, yeah, thanks. Mr. MacKade. The ice cream was great. Come on, Con."

"Thanks, Mr. MacKade." Since Emma already had his hand and was tugging on it, Connor slid from the booth. He looked down at his sister, wrinkled his brow.

"Thank you," she said, keeping an iron grip on her brother's hand.

"You're welcome. Say hi to Regan."

"We will. Mama," Connor called out, "we're going down to Regan's."

"Don't touch anything," Cassie told them, balancing two plates on one arm and serving another. "And come right back if she's busy."

"Yes'm."

Bryan was already out of the door, and Connor followed, hampered by his sister's sedate pace.

"I'd say you hit a home run," Savannah commented, leaning back to drape an arm over the back of the booth.

"You hit one yourself. That's one of the longest conversations I've ever heard out of Emma."

"It must be hard, being shy. She looks like an angel. Like her mother."

Angels who'd already been through hell, Jared thought. "Cassie's doing a terrific job with them, on her own. You'd appreciate that."

"Yes, I would." Savannah glanced over to where Cassie was busy wiping down a booth. "You're... close?"

"I've known her most of my life, but no, not the way you mean. She's a friend." Pleased she was interested enough to ask, he took out a cigar. "And a client.

Anything beyond friendship wouldn't be ethical, when I'm representing her."

"And you'd be a very ethical man, wouldn't you, Lawyer MacKade?"

"That's right. You know, you've never mentioned what you do."

"About what?"

"About making a living."

"I've done all sorts of things." With a sizzling look, she took the cigar from him.

"I'll just bet you have," he murmured.

"Right now I'm an illustrator. Kids' books, mostly." Laughing, she passed the cigar back to him. "Doesn't quite fit the image, does it?"

"I don't know. I'd have to see some of your illustrations." He glanced up, and his lips curved. "Hey, Dev."

Savannah shifted to see the man who had just come in. He had the same dark, go-to-hell looks as Jared, a body that was tall and tough and rangy. The eyes were green, as well, but they were different.

She recognized the way they swept the room, checked for details, looked for trouble. Instinctively her muscles tightened, her face went blank. She didn't need the badge on his chest to tell her this was the sheriff. She could spot a cop at half a mile on a speeding horse. She could smell one at twenty paces.

"Saw your car." After one quick scan of the room, one quick smile for Cassie, Devin dropped into the booth beside his brother.

"Savannah Morningstar, Devin MacKade."

"Nice to meet you." An eyeful was Devin's first impression. Then he caught the chill, and wondered about it. "You bought the cabin? The doctor's place."

"That's right. It's my place now."

Not just a chill, he mused. Ice was forming. "That must be your kid I've run into out at the farm Bryan, right?"

"Yes, Bryan's my son. He's well fed, he's in school, and he's had his shots. Excuse me, I'd better go see what the kids are up to."

And straight into frostbite, Devin mused as she slid from the booth. He winced as the door swung to behind her. "Ouch. What the hell was that about?"

"I don't know," Jared murmured. "But I'm going to find out." He pulled bills out of his pocket.

"You want a guess?" Devin made way so that Jared could climb out of the booth. "The lady's had trouble with the law."

Damn, damn, damn. On the sidewalk, Savannah struggled to regain her composure. That had been stupid, she berated herself. That had been foolish. The trouble with letting yourself relax, she reminded herself, was that all sorts of nasty things could sneak up and bite you in the back.

Now that she was outside, her fists jammed into the snug pockets of her jeans, she realized that she didn't know what this Regan's shop was, much less where it was. All she wanted was to get her son and take him home.

"You want to tell me what just happened?" Jared stepped up behind her, touched a hand to her shoulder.

Savannah made herself take a careful breath before turning. "I finished my ice cream."

"Then maybe you should walk it off." He twined his fingers around her arm and had them quickly and fiercely shaken off.

"Don't take hold of me unless I ask you."

He felt the MacKade temper stir and clamped down on it. "Fine. Why don't you tell me why you were rude?"

"I'm often rude," she shot back. "Especially to cops. I don't like cops. They're one step down from lawyers.

I'm not interested in socializing with either one. Which way are the kids?"

"It seems to me we were just socializing up a storm."

"Now we're not. Go back and talk law and order with your brother." The old fury, the old fears, wouldn't quite let go. "You can tell him to go ahead and run a make on me. I'm clean. I have valid employment, and money in the bank."

"Good for you," Jared said equably. "Why should Devin run a make on you?"

"Because cops and lawyers love to stick their noses in other people's business. That's what you've been doing with me ever since you drove up my lane. The way I live and the way I raise my son are my concern and nobody else's. So back off."

It was fascinating. Even through his own bubbling temper, it was fascinating to watch her simmer and spew. "I haven't gotten in your way yet, Savannah. You'll know when I do. Believe me, you'll know. Right now, I'm just asking for an explanation."

She didn't know how he did it. How he could look searing daggers at her and still speak in that controlled, reasonable voice. She hated people who could manage that.

"You've just got the only one I'm giving. Now where's my son?"

Jared kept his eyes on hers. "Past Times—two doors behind you." But when she started to whirl away, he took her arm again.

"I told you not to—"

"You listen to me. You're not going to charge in there like some fire-breathing Amazon."

The heat in her eyes could have boiled the skin off a man. "You'd better take your hand off me before I damage that pretty face of yours."

He only tightened his grip. Under different circumstances, he might have enjoyed seeing her try. "There are two abused kids in that shop," he began, and watched her face change. Fury to surprise, surprise to painful sympathy.

"Connor and Emma. I should have seen it." Her gaze darted to the wide glass window of Ed's. "Cassandra."

"Those kids watched their mother get beaten by their father, and that's more violence in those two short lives than anyone deserves. You go storming in there, you'll—"

"I don't make a habit of frightening children," Savannah snapped back. "Whatever you by-the-book types think, I'm a good mother. Bryan's never done without. He's had the best I could give him, and—"

She shut her eyes and fought back the rage. Jared thought it was like watching a volcano capping itself.

"Let go of my arm," she said, calmly now. "I'm going to take my son home."

Jared studied her face another moment, saw the licks of temper just behind the molten brown of her eyes. He released her, watched her walk to Regan's shop, take one more calming breath before pulling open the door and going inside.

Devin strolled out. He stopped beside Jared and scratched his head. "That was quite an interesting show."

"I have a feeling it was just the overture." Intrigued, Jared tucked his hands in his pockets, rocked back on his heels. "There's a lot going on in there."

"A woman like that could make a man forget his own name." With a faint smile, Devin looked over at his brother. "You remember yours?"

"Yeah, just barely. I think you were right about her having problems with the law."

Devin's eyes narrowed. The law, the town and everyone in it were his responsibility. "I could run a make on her."

"No, don't do that. It's just what she expects." Thoughtfully Jared turned toward his car. "I've got an urge to give the lady the unexpected. We'll see what happens."

"Your call," Devin murmured as Jared climbed behind the wheel. Your call, he thought again. As long as the lady stays out of trouble.

Bryan stared out the car window, his face averted coolly from his mother's. He didn't see why Connor couldn't spend the night. It was still Saturday, and there were hours and hours left until the dumb bell rang for school on lousy Monday.

What was a guy supposed to do with all those hours without his best bud? Chores, he thought, rolling his dark brown eyes. Homework. Might as well be in jail.

"Might as well be in jail," he said aloud, turning his face now in challenge.

"Yeah, they play a lot of baseball, eat a lot of butterscotch sundaes, in the joint."

"But I've got nothing to do at home," he said—the desperate lament of every nine-year-old.

"I'll give you something to do," Savannah shot

back—the typical response of every frustrated parent. And when she heard that come out of her mouth she nearly groaned. "I'm sorry, Bry, I've got a lot on my mind, and it's just not a good night for a sleep-over."

"I could've stayed at Con's. *His* mother wouldn't care."

Direct hit, she thought grimly as she turned up the lane. "Well, yours does, Ace, and you're stuck with me. You can start by taking out the trash you didn't take out this morning, cleaning that black hole that passes as your room, then studying your math so you don't end up in summer school."

"Great." The minute she stopped the car, he slammed out. He muttered another comment about it being worse than jail that had smoke coming out of her ears.

"Bryan Morningstar." His name lashed out. When he pivoted back, they stood glaring at each other, angry color riding high on each set of cheekbones, eyes almost black with passionate temper. "Why the hell are you so much like me?" she demanded. She threw her face up to the sun. "I could have had a nice, quiet, well-mannered little girl if I'd tried really hard. Why did I think I'd like having some snotty, bad-tempered boy with big feet?"

It made his lips twitch. "Because then you'd have to take out the trash yourself. A girl would whine and say it was too messy."

"I could take the trash out," she said consideringly. "In fact, I think I will, after I put you in it." She made a grab, but he danced back, laughing at her.

"You're too old to catch me."

"Oh, yeah?" She streaked forward, pounded up the bank after him. He stood hooting at her, taunting. Which was his mistake. She snagged him, making the catch more from her advantage of reach and experience than from speed, and tumbled with him to the grass.

"Who's old, smart mouth?"

"You are." He shrieked with laughter as her fingers dug mercilessly into his ribs. "You're almost thirty."

"I am not. Take it back." She whipped him into a headlock, rubbed her knuckles over his hair. "Take it back, and do the math, Einstein. What's twenty-six from thirty?"

"Nothing," he shouted. "Zero." Then, fearing he might wet his pants if she kept tickling, he surrendered. "It's four, okay? It's four."

"Remember that. And remember who can still take you down." She pulled him back against her, hugged him so suddenly, so fiercely, he blinked. "I love you, Bryan. I love you so much."

"Jeez, Mom." He wriggled in mortification. "I know."

"I'm sorry I snapped at you."

He rolled his eyes, but trickles of remorse found their way through the embarrassment. "I guess I'm sorry, too."

"You and Connor can have a sleep-over next weekend. I promise."

"Okay, that's cool." When she didn't release him, he frowned. But it wasn't so bad, letting her hold him—since none of the guys were around to see. She smelled nice, and her arms were soft. There were flickers of memory of being rocked and soothed.

He was simply too young to do anything but take them for granted. She'd always been there. She always would. He let his head rest on her shoulder, and didn't feel like squirming when she stroked his hair.

"Could we maybe cook out on the grill later?"

"Sure. Want superburgers?"

"Yeah, and french fries."

"What's a superburger without fries?" she murmured, then sighed. "Bryan, has Con said anything to you about his father?"

She felt her son go still, and pressed a light kiss to his hair. "Is it a secret?"

"Sort of."

"I don't want you to betray a confidence. I found out today that Connor's father used to hit his mother. I thought if Con had talked to you about it, you might want to talk to me."

He'd wanted to, ever since Connor had told him. But Connor had cried some—even though Bryan had pretended not to notice. And a guy just didn't tell his mother things like that.

"Con's said he's in jail for hitting her. Con said he used to hurt her real bad, and he drank a lot and gave her bruises and everything. They're getting divorced."

"I see." She'd seen plenty of men who were Joe Dolin's type in her life, but that didn't stop her from despising them. "Did he hit Con, too? And Emma?"

"Not Emma." Here was another dicey part, but Bryan heard himself blurting it out before he could stop. "But he hit Con. Not when his mom was around and could see. He'd call him names and shove him. He said Con was a sissy 'cause he liked to read books and write stories. Con's no sissy."

"Of course he's not."

"He's just real smart. He doesn't hardly have to study to get the answers right. But he doesn't raise his hand in class very much. The teacher calls on him anyway." As he stared off into the woods, Bryan's face darkened with rage. "Some of the kids give him a hard time about things. About his father, and how he's teacher's pet and how he can't throw a baseball very far. But they back off when I'm around."

Savannah closed her eyes, laid one cheek on Bryan's head. "You're quite a guy."

"Hell—heck." He corrected himself quickly. "Bullies are just wimps underneath, right?"

"Right. Con's not the only one who's smart." She let out a sigh. "Bryan, I need to talk to you. Do you remember the other day, when you came home and Mr. MacKade was here?"

"Sure."

"He's a lawyer, and he came here on business."

"Are we in trouble?"

"No." She turned him so that they were face-to-face. "We're not in trouble. We're fine. He came about… My father died, Bryan."

"Oh." He felt nothing but mild surprise himself. He'd never met his grandfather, knew of him only because his mother had explained that Jim Morningstar was a rodeo rider who moved around a lot. "I guess he was pretty old."

"Yeah." Fifty? she wondered. Sixty? She didn't have a clue. "I never really explained things to you, exactly. Your grandfather and I had a fight a long time ago, and I left home."

How could she tell this child, her beautiful child, that he'd been the cause of it? No, that she wouldn't do. That she would never do.

"Anyway, I left, and we sort of lost touch."

"How did Mr. MacKade know he was dead? Did he know him?"

"No, it's a lawyer thing. Your grandfather got hurt, and it started him thinking, I guess. He hired this lawyer out in Oklahoma to find us, and the lawyer called Mr. MacKade. It all took a while, then Mr. MacKade came out to tell me. And to let me know that your grandfather left some money."

"Wow, really?"

"It's about seven thousand—"

"Dollars?" Bryan finished for her, eyes popping. It was all the money in the world. Enough for a new bike, a new mitt, the Cal Ripkin rookie baseball card he lusted for. "We get to keep it? Just like that?"

"I have to sign some papers."

The dollar signs faded from his eyes long enough for Bryan to read his mother's face. "How come you don't want it?"

"I… Oh, Bryan." Defeated, she curled up her legs and rested her brow on them. "I don't know how to explain it to you. I've been so mad at him all these years. Now I'm mad at him for waiting until he was dead."

Bryan patted her head and thought it over. "Is it like him saying he's sorry? And if you take it you'd be saying you were sorry, too?"

She let out a half laugh at the simplicity of it. "Why couldn't I have thought of that?" Wearily she lifted her head, studied his face. "You think we should take it."

"I guess we don't need to." He watched Cal Ripkin fly gracefully away. "I mean, you've got your job, and we've got a house now."

"No," she murmured. "We don't need to." She felt the weight slip from her shoulders. They didn't need to, and that was exactly why they could. "I'll go see Mr. MacKade on Monday and tell him to put the money through."

"Cool." Bryan leaped to his feet. "I'm going to call Con and tell him we're rich."

"No."

He skidded to a halt. "But, Mom…"

"No. Bragging about money is very uncool. And I might as well break it to you now, Ace. It doesn't make us rich, and I'm dumping it into a college fund."

His mouth dropped open, nearly scraping his shoes. "College? That's a hundred years away. Maybe I won't even go."

"That'll be up to you, but the money'll be there."

"Oh, man." At nine, Bryan was experiencing the pain of a fortune won and lost. "All of it?"

"All—" his shattered face changed her mind in midstep "—except some. You can have one thing. It'll be like a present from your grandfather."

Hope bloomed. "One anything?"

"One any reasonable thing. A gold-plated Corvette slides over to the unreasonable side."

He let out a whoop, leaped over to hug her. "I've gotta go look up something in my baseball-card price guide."

She watched him go, full steam, catapulting onto the porch, streaking into the house with the screen door slamming like a gunshot behind him.

* * *

Later, while she grilled burgers on the porch with Bryan curled up with his price guide and dreams of glory, Jared sat on the other side of the haunted woods and thought of her.

He was tempted, very tempted, to stride through those woods and finish the altercation she had started that afternoon out on the sidewalk in front of Ed's.

Prickly women weren't his style, Jared reminded himself and set the chair rocking. Prickly women with lightning tempers and murky pasts were even less so. Not that she wasn't interesting, and not that he didn't like fitting puzzle pieces together.

But his life was cruising along at a very comfortable pace at the moment. He would have enjoyed her companionship—on a purely superficial level, of course. A few dates, leading to physical contact. After all, a dead man would fantasize about rolling around with a woman who looked like that.

And Jared MacKade wasn't dead.

He also wasn't stupid. The woman who'd blasted him that afternoon was nothing but trouble. The last thing one hot temper needed was to crash up against another. That was why he preferred his women cool, composed and reasonable.

Like his ex-wife, he thought with a grimace. She'd been so cool there were times he wanted to hold a mirror in front of her mouth to see if she was still breathing.

But that was another story.

First thing Monday morning, he was going to draft a nice formal letter advising Savannah Morningstar of her inheritance and the steps she was required to take to accept or decline it.

He didn't mind getting his hands dirty for a client, sweating for one, even losing sleep for one. But she wasn't his damn client, and he'd taken professional courtesy to his colleague out west as far as he intended to.

He was out of it.

Hell, the woman had a kid. A very appealing kid, but that was beside the point. If he pursued a personal relationship with her, it would involve the kid, as well. There was no way around that one and, Jared admitted, there shouldn't be one.

Then there was that fact that, beneath that scorching beauty, the woman was tough as shoe leather. There was no doubt that she'd been around, knew the ropes and had probably climbed plenty of them. A woman didn't get eyes that aware by spending all her time baking biscuits.

He imagined she could chew a man up, spit him out, and have him come crawling back for more.

Well, not this man.

He could handle her, of course. If he wanted to.

That exotic, unbelievable face zipped straight to the center of his mind and taunted him.

God, he wanted to.

In disgust, Jared sprang up and headed into the woods. He needed to walk, he decided. And he preferred the company of ghosts to his own thoughts.

Chapter 4

"Good afternoon, MacKade law offices." Sissy Bleaker, Jared's secretary, answered the phone on the fly. It was quarter to five, she had a hot date in exactly one hour, and the boss had been like a bear with a sore tooth all day. "Oh, yes, hello, Mr. Brill. No, Mr. MacKade is in conference."

Sissy could have spit nails when the front door opened. How the devil was she supposed to look irresistibly sexy in an hour if she couldn't get out of here?

"I'll be happy to take a message." As she picked up a pad, she glanced up. And decided she could have a week at her disposal and not pull off the kind of in-your-face sexy that had just walked into Jared MacKade's outer office.

Savannah hated being here. She hated that she'd felt obliged to change out of jeans into pleated trousers and a jacket. Something about visiting official places compelled her to put on a front.

And this place certainly looked official. The pretty plants and bland pastel paintings on matte-white walls didn't hide the fact that law was the order here. The carpet was a muted gray, the deeper-toned chairs in the waiting area were likely just the wrong side of comfortable.

We wouldn't want people to be at their ease now, would we? she thought bitterly.

She'd never known a den of authority—social services, a principal's office, an unemployment line—to offer comfort. Still, she'd thought the man had more style than to choose such a cold, formal setting for his work.

The secretary behind the polished reception-area desk was young, bright-eyed and, Savannah was sure, fiercely efficient. The quick greeting smile she sent in Savannah's direction was carefully empty of curiosity and perfectly balanced between warm and cool.

Savannah had no idea Sissy was curdling with envy inside.

"Yes, Mr. Brill, I'll see that he gets your message. You're welcome. Goodbye." Wondering just where the mystery visitor had come across that terrific jacket, all sweeping lines and bold colors, Sissy hung up the phone and aimed her most professional smile.

"Good afternoon. May I help you?"

"I'd like to see Mr. MacKade."

"Do you have an appointment?" Sissy knew very well she did not. Jared's schedule was filed in her brain right alongside her own.

"No, I was…" Damn, she hated this. "I was in town, and I thought I'd take a chance he'd be free for a minute."

"I'm afraid he's in conference, Ms.…"

"Morningstar." Of course he was in conference, Savannah thought nastily. Where else was a lawyer when he wasn't on the putting green but in conference? "Then I'd like to leave a message."

The name Morningstar rang all sorts of bells in Sissy's brain. It had been said through gritted teeth that morning, when Jared dictated a briskly formal letter with all kinds of interesting hums between the lines.

"Certainly. If it's personal, you could write it down and I'll... Oh." Sissy beamed at her phone. "Mr. MacKade's just finished his conference call, I see. Why don't I buzz him, see if he can squeeze you in?"

"Fine, great." Restless, Savannah turned away to pace.

Sissy decided that if she grew six inches in height, filled out several more in the right places, she might just look that impressive on the move.

"Mr. MacKade, there's a Ms. Morningstar to see you, if you have a moment. Yes, sir, she's in the office now. Yes, sir." Careful to keep her lips from sliding into a smile, Sissy hung up the phone. "He'll see you, Ms. Morningstar. It's right up those stairs and to the left. First door."

"Thanks." Savannah turned toward the short curve of stairs, put one hand on the pristine white rail and climbed.

Must have been a town house at one time, she decided. Or a duplex. Though she wouldn't have called the place homey, Savannah admitted it had class—if you went in for snooty and nondescript.

There was a short hallway at the top of the steps, a print of a spray of white orchids in a white vase that was so soulless and ordinary it offended her artist's eye, and two doors facing each other.

She strode to the one on the left, rapped once and opened it.

Of course he'd look terrific in charcoal gray, she thought. A lot better than the office did, with its dull grays and punishing whites. Someone should tell him work was more pleasant in an environment with a little color and life.

But it wouldn't be her.

He rose, elegant in his three-piece suit and carefully knotted tie. A tie he'd just jerked back into place. She thought, with an inner sense of rebellion, that he looked like more of a lawyer than ever.

"Ms. Morningstar." He inclined his head. He thought that her stepping into the room was like having some brilliant bolt of lightning strike a placid pond. "Have a seat."

"It won't take long." She remained standing, stubbornly. "I appreciate you taking the time to see me."

"I had the time." To illustrate the point, he moved a file from the center of his desk to the side, and sat. "What can I do for you?"

In answer, she pulled papers out of her purse, tossed

them on his desk. "I signed them, in triplicate, and had them notarized." Her driver's license landed with a plop on top of the papers. "That's my ID." She threw in her social security card for good measure. "I don't have a birth certificate."

"Mm-hmm…" Taking his time, Jared pulled brown horn-rims out of his jacket pocket and slipped them on to study the papers.

Savannah stared at him, swallowed hard. It didn't seem to matter that she told herself it was ridiculous. Her heart *had* skipped a beat. He looked gorgeous, intellectually sexy, in those damn glasses. And made her feel like a fumbling fool.

"It's all in order," she began.

"Afraid not." Thoughtfully, he picked up her driver's license, perused it. "This is invalid."

"The hell it is. I just had it renewed a couple of months ago."

"That may be," he continued, studying her now. "But as the picture actually looks like you, and is, in fact, flattering, this driver's license is obviously a fraud, and therefore, invalid."

She closed her mouth, jammed her hands in her

pockets. "Are you making a joke? Is that allowed in hallowed halls?"

"Sit down, Savannah. Please."

With a bad-tempered shrug, she sat. "Did you ever hear of color?" she demanded. "This place is dull as a textbook, and your art is pathetically ordinary."

"It is, isn't it?" he agreed easily. "My ex-wife decorated the place. She was a tax accountant, had the office across the hall." He leaned back and scanned the room. "I've gotten used to not seeing the place, but you're right. It could use something."

"It could use an obituary." Annoyed with herself, she pushed a hand through her hair. "I hate being here."

"I can see that." He picked up the papers again, skimmed through them. "You understand that you're agreeing to accept a payment, by cashier's check, that equals the total cash balance of your father's estate?"

"Yes."

"And his effects?"

"I thought…I thought that meant the money. What else is there?"

"Apparently there are a few personal effects. I can get you an itemized list if you like, so that you can decide if you want them sent or discarded. The shipping would be deducted from the estate."

Discarded, she thought. As she had been. "No, just have them sent."

"All right." Methodically he made notes on a yellow legal pad. "I'll have my secretary draft a letter tomorrow confirming the status and apprising you that you'll receive full disbursement of the estate within forty-five days."

"Why do you need a letter when you've just told me?"

He glanced up from the papers, the eyes behind the lenses amused. "The law likes to cover its butt with as much paperwork as humanly possible."

He signed the papers himself as proxy for his colleague, then handed Savannah back her license and social security card.

"That's it, then?"

"That's it."

"Well." Feeling awkward, and relieved, she rose. "It wasn't as painful as I expected. I suppose if I'm ever in the market for a lawyer, I'll give you a call."

"I wouldn't have you as a client, Savannah."

Her eyes fired as he took off his glasses and stood to come around the desk. "That's very neighborly of you."

"I wouldn't have you as a client," he repeated, standing behind her, "because then this would be unethical."

He caught her off guard. She'd had no idea any man could still catch her off guard. But she was in Jared's arms and being thoroughly kissed before she had a chance to evade.

If she'd wanted to evade.

There was heat, of course. She expected that, enjoyed that. But it was the lushness of it that surprised her—the silky, sumptuous spread of it that bloomed in that meeting of lips, flowering through her body.

He held her close, in a smooth, confident embrace, no fumbling, no grappling. He gave her room to resist, and as that clever, wide-palmed hand skimmed lightly up her spine, she thought only a fool would step away from that caress, that mouth, that heat.

So she stepped into it, sliding her own hands up his back until they were hooked over his shoulders.

He'd wondered what he would find here. From the moment she stood, clumps of flowers at her feet, and looked at him, he'd wondered. Now he knew there was strength in those long, lovely arms, fire in that soft, full mouth. She opened for him as if he'd touched her hundreds of times, and her taste was gloriously familiar. The press of her body against his, every firm, generous curve, was an erotic homecoming.

He tangled his fingers in her hair, slowly tugging her head back to savor. And as her mouth moved warm on his, he discovered what it was to be savored in turn.

Gradually, thoughtfully, he drew back to study her face. Her eyes were steady, calm. Darker, yes, he mused. He knew by the way her heart had jumped against his that whatever had moved through him had moved through her, as well. But she didn't tremble.

What would it take to make a woman like this tremble?

He knew he would have to discover that secret, and all the others she kept hidden behind those dark, unreadable eyes.

"But," he said, "I can certainly recommend a lawyer for you, if you find you need one."

She lifted a brow. Oh, he was a cool one, she thought, carrying on the conversation as if her insides weren't sizzling. Appreciating it, she smiled. "Why, thank you."

"Excuse me a minute," he said when his phone rang. "Yes, Sissy." His gaze left Savannah's only long enough for a glance at his watch. "So it is," he murmured, noting that it was just after five. "You go ahead, I'll lock up. And, Sissy, the letter I dictated this morning. The first letter? Yes. Don't mail that. I need to make some changes."

Savannah watched him consideringly. He was sending his secretary off for the day, and they would be alone. She understood what it meant when a man looked at a woman the way Jared was looking at her. She understood what happened between men and women after they'd shared a mutually lusty kiss.

Over the years, she'd learned to be very careful, very…selective. The responsibility of raising a child alone wasn't a small one. Men could come and go, but her son was forever. She wasn't a woman who stepped blindly into affairs, who scratched every itch or accepted every advance.

But she was also realistic. The man currently dismissing his secretary, the man flipping through his daily calendar to coordinate his schedule, was about to become her lover.

"My secretary's got a date," Jared commented when he hung up the phone. "So it looks like we're closing the office on time today." Tilting his head, he studied

Savannah. "I'm supposed to ask you, discreetly, where you got your jacket."

"My jacket?" Bemused, Savannah glanced down. "I made it."

"You're kidding."

Her bottom lip moved into an expression somewhere between a pout and a sneer, and her chin rose in a gesture he now recognized as an indicator of temper simmering. "What? I don't look like the type who can sew? I don't fit the happy-homemaker image?"

Intrigued, he rested a hip on the edge of his desk, reached out to rub the brilliantly hued lapel of her jacket between his fingers. "Nice work. What else can you do?"

"Whatever I need to do." She didn't bother to protest when he tugged her toward him. Instead, she rested her hands on his shoulders and leaned down into the kiss.

"It's early," he murmured.

"Relatively."

"Where's Bryan?"

"At Cassie's." Mildly surprised he'd bothered to ask, she changed the angle of the kiss and let herself sink in. "I'm going to pick him up about six. I've got about a half an hour."

"It's going to take longer." He shifted, took her by the hips and drew her intimately between his legs. "Why don't you call her and see if he can stay until seven?" His teeth nipped gently over that lovely bottom lip. "Seven-thirty."

She was going to enjoy getting him out of that tie, Savannah thought. "I suppose I could."

"Good. You clear it, then we'll go across the street."

"Across the street?"

"For an early dinner."

She drew back, stared at him. "Dinner?"

"Yes." Almost certain his legs would support him, Jared stood, before he could give in to the urge to tear off her clothes, drag her to the floor and have her. "I'd like to take you to dinner."

"Why?"

"Because I'd enjoy spending an hour or two with you." On top of you, he thought. Inside you. God. With every appearance of calm, he skirted the desk and flipped through his address file. "Here's Cassie's number."

"I know Cassie's number." It was demoralizing to realize she had to take a good, deep breath to steady herself, when he was just standing there, so coolly, so easily. "What's going on here, Jared? We both know dinner isn't necessary."

His stomach twisted into tight slick knots. He could take her. Right here, right now. It was just that simple. And anything too simple was suspect.

"I'd like to have dinner with you, Savannah. And conversation." Picking up the phone, he dialed Cassie's number himself, held out the receiver. "All right?"

Filled with mistrust, she hesitated. With a shrug, she took the phone. "All right."

The restaurant was casual, the menu basic American grill. Savannah toyed with her drink and waited for Jared's next move.

"So, you make clothes."

"Sometimes."

Smiling, he leaned back in the wooden booth. "Sometimes?" he repeated, looking at her expectantly.

He wanted to make conversation, she determined. She could make conversation. "I learned because homemade is cheaper than store-bought, and I didn't want to be naked. Now I make something now and again because I enjoy it."

"But you make your living as an illustrator, not as a seamstress."

"I like to work with color, and design. I got lucky."

"Lucky?"

Wary of the friendly probing, she moved her shoulders. "You don't want the story of my life, Jared."

"But I do." He smiled at the waitress who set their meals in front of them. "Start anywhere," he said invitingly.

She shook her head, cut into the spicy blackened chicken he'd recommended. "You've lived here all your life, haven't you?"

"That's right."

"Big family, old friends and neighbors. Roots."

"Yeah."

"I'm going to give my son roots. Not just a roof over his head, but roots."

He was silent for a moment. There had been a fierceness in her voice, a fiery determination, that he had to admire, even as he wondered at it. "Why here?"

"Because it's not the West. That's first. I wanted to get away from the dust, the plains, and all those sunbaked little towns. That was for me," she admitted. "I've been moving east for ten years. This seemed far enough."

When he said nothing, she relaxed a little. It was difficult to combat that quiet way he had of listening. "I didn't want the city for Bryan. But I wanted to give him a sense of belonging, of…"

"Community?"

"Yeah. Small town, kids, people who'd get to know him by name. But I still wanted a little distance. That was for me again. And…"

"And?"

"I was drawn here," she said at length. "Maybe it's the mysticism in my blood and my heritage, but I felt—I knew that this would be home. The land, the hills. The woods. Your woods called to me." Amused at herself, she smiled. "How's that for weird?"

"They've called to me all my life," Jared said, so simply her smile faded. "I could never be happy anywhere else. I moved to the city because it seemed practical. And small towns and long walks through the woods weren't my ex-wife's style."

If he could probe, so could she. "Why did you marry her?"

"Because it seemed practical." Now it was his turn

to wince. "Which doesn't say much for either of us. We were reasonably attracted, respected each other, and entered into a very civilized, intelligent and totally passionless contract of marriage. Two years later, we had a very civilized, intelligent and totally passionless divorce."

It was difficult, all but impossible, to visualize the man who had kissed her being passionless about anything. "No blood spilled?"

"Absolutely not. We were both much too reasonable for combat. There were no children." Her choice, he remembered, only slightly bitter. "She'd kept her own name."

"A modern professional marriage."

"You've got it. We split everything down the middle and went our separate ways. No harm, no foul."

Curious, Savannah tilted her head. "It bothered you that she didn't take your name."

He started to correct her, then shrugged. "Yeah, it bothered me. Not very modern or professional of me. Just one of those things that would have made the commitment emotional instead of reasonable. That's just pride."

"Partly," Savannah agreed. "But part of you wanted

to give her that piece of you that you were most proud of, that had been passed to you, and that you wanted to pass to your children."

"You're astute," he murmured.

"Lawyers aren't the only ones who can read people. And I understand the importance of names. When Bryan was born, I stared at the form they give you. For names. And I thought, what do I put where it says Father? If I put the name down, then I'm giving that name to my son. My son," she repeated quietly.

"What did you put down?"

She brought herself back from that moment, when she'd been barely seventeen, and alone. Completely alone. "Unknown," she said. "Because he'd stopped being important. My name was enough."

"He's never seen Bryan?"

"No. He packed up his gear and lit out like a rocket the day I told him I was pregnant. Don't say you're sorry," she said, anticipating him. "He did me a favor. It's easy for a sixteen-year-old girl to be dreamy-eyed and hot-blooded over a good-looking cowboy, but it isn't easy to live with one."

"What have you told Bryan?"

"The truth. I always tell him the truth—or as close to

it as I can without hurting him. I'm not ashamed that I was once foolish enough to imagine myself in love. And I'm grateful that sometimes foolishness is rewarded by something as spectacular as Bryan."

"You're a remarkable woman."

It touched and embarrassed her that he should think so. "No, I'm a lucky one."

"It couldn't have been easy."

"I don't need things to be easy."

He considered that, and thought it was more that she didn't care for things to be easy. That he understood.

"What did you do when you left home?"

"When I got kicked out," she said. "You don't have to pretty it up. My father gave me the back of his hand, called me...all sorts of things it's impolite to repeat to a man wearing such a nice suit—and showed me the door. Wasn't much of a door," she remembered, surprised to see that Jared had reached out to link his fingers with hers. "We were living in a trailer at the time."

He was appalled. Probably shouldn't be, he realized. He'd heard stories as bad, and worse, in his own office. But he was appalled at the image of Savannah at sixteen, pregnant and facing the world alone.

"Didn't you have anyone you could go to?"

"No, there was no one. I didn't know my mother's family. He'd have probably changed his mind in a day or two. He was like that. But the things he'd called me had hurt a lot more than the slap, so I put on my backpack, stuck out my thumb, and didn't look back. Got a job waiting tables in Oklahoma City." She picked up her drink. "That's probably why Cassie and I hit it off. We both know what it's like to stand on your feet all day and serve people. But she does a better job of it."

Oh, there was plenty she was skimming over, Jared thought. Miles of road she wasn't taking him over. "How did you get from waiting tables in Oklahoma City to illustrating children's books?"

"By taking a lot of detours." Well fed, she leaned back and smiled at him. "You'd be surprised at some of the things I've done." Her smile widened at his bland look. "Oh, yes, you would."

"Name some."

"Served drinks to drunks in a dive in Wichita."

"You're going to have to do better than that, if you want to shock me."

"Worked a strip joint in Abilene. There." She chuckled and plucked the thin cigar he'd just taken out of his pocket from his fingers. "That's got you thinking."

Determined not to goggle, he struck a match, held it to the tip of the cigar when she leaned over. "You were a stripper."

"Exotic dancer." She blew out smoke and grinned. "You are shocked."

"I'm...intrigued."

"Mm-hmm... To pop the fantasy a bit, I never got down to the bare essentials. You'd see women on the beach wearing about as much as I shook down to— only I got paid for it. Not terribly well." Casually she handed him back the cigar. "I made more money designing and sewing costumes for the other girls than I did peeling out of them. So I retired from the stage."

"You're leaving out chunks, Savannah."

"That's right." They were her business. "Let's say I didn't like the hours. I worked a dog and pony show for a while."

"A dog and pony show."

"A poor man's circus. Took a breather in New Orleans selling paintings of bayous and street scenes, and doing charcoal sketches of tourists. I liked it. Great food, great music."

"But you didn't stay," he pointed out.

"I never stayed long in one place. Habit. Just about

the time I was getting restless, I got lucky. One of the tourists who sat for me was a writer. Kids' books. She'd just ditched her illustrator. Creative differences, she said. She liked my work and offered me a deal. I'd read her manuscript and do a few illustrations. If her publisher went for it, I'd have a job. If not, she'd pay me a hundred for my time. How could I lose?"

"You got the job."

"I got a life," she told him. "The kind where I didn't have to leave Bryan with sitters, worry about how I was going to pay the rent that month, or if the social workers were going to come knocking to check me out and decide if I was a fit mother. The kind where cops don't roust you to see if you're selling paintings or yourself. After a while, I had enough put together that I could buy my son a yard, a nice school, Little League games. A community." She tipped back her glass again. "And here we are."

"And here we are," he repeated. "Where do you suppose we're going?"

"That's a question I'll have to ask you. Why are we having dinner and conversation instead of sex?"

To his credit, he didn't choke, but blew out smoke smoothly. "That's blunt."

"Lawyers like to use twenty words when one will do," she countered. "I don't."

"Then let's just say you expected sex. I don't like being predictable." Behind the haze of smoke, his eyes flashed on hers with a power that jarred. "When we get around to sex, Savannah, it won't be predictable. You'll know exactly who you're with, and you'll remember it."

In that moment, she didn't have the slightest doubt. Perhaps that was what worried her. "All your moves, Lawyer MacKade? Your time and place?"

"That's right." His eyes changed, lightened with a humor that was hard to resist. "I'm a traditional kind of guy."

Chapter 5

A traditional kind of guy, Savannah mused. One day after her impromptu dinner with Jared, and she was standing in her kitchen, her hands on her hips, staring at the florist's box.

He'd sent her roses. A dozen long-stemmed red beauties.

Traditional, certainly. Even predictable, in their way, she supposed. Unless you factored in that no one in her life had ever sent her a long, glossy white box filled with red roses.

She was certain he knew it.

Then there was the card.

* * *

Until your garden blooms

How did he know flowers were one of her biggest weaknesses, that she had pined for bright, fragrant blooms in those years when she was living in tiny, cramped rooms in noisy, crowded cities? That she'd promised herself that one day she would have a garden of her own, planted and tended by her own hands?

Because he saw too much, she decided, and circled the flowers as warily as a dog circling a stranger. She was so intent on them, she actually jumped when the phone rang. Cursing herself she yanked up the receiver.

"Yes. Hello."

"Bad time?" Jared asked.

She scowled at the flowers lying beautifully against the green protective paper. "I'm busy, if that's what you mean."

"Then I won't keep you. I thought you might like to bring Bryan over to the farm for dinner tonight."

Still frowning, she reached into the box, took out a single rose. It didn't bite. "Why?"

"Why not?"

"For starters, I've already got sauce on for spaghetti."

She waited a beat. So did he. "I suppose you expect me to ask you to come here to dinner."

"Yep."

Twirling the rose, she tried to think of a good reason not to. "All right. But Bryan has baseball practice after school. I have to pick him up at six, so—"

"I'll pick him up. It's on my way. See you tonight, then."

Something seemed to be slipping out of her hands. "I told you all of this wasn't necessary," she muttered. "The flowers."

"Do you like them?"

"Sure, they're beautiful."

"Well, then." That seemed to settle the matter. "I'll see you a bit after six."

Befuddled, she hung up. After another long stare at the roses, she decided she'd better dig up a vase.

At six-fifteen she heard the sound of a car coming up her lane. Carefully she finished a detail on the illustration of her wicked queen for a reissue of traditional fairy tales, then turned away from her worktable. Bryan was already clattering up the steps by the time she walked from her small studio into the kitchen.

"...then he popped up, and that klutzoid Tommy couldn't get his glove under it. His mom had two cows when the ball came down and smacked him in the face. Blood was spurting out of his nose. It was so cool. Hi, Mom."

"Bryan." She lifted a brow at the state of his clothes. Red dirt streaked every inch. "Do some sliding today?"

"Yeah." He headed straight to the refrigerator for a jug of juice.

"Tommy Mardson got a bloody nose," Jared put in.

"So I hear."

"His mom was really screaming." Excited by the memory, Bryan nearly forgot to bother with a glass—until he caught his own mother's steely eye. "It wasn't broke. Just smashed real good."

"We're going to work on that grammar tonight, Ace."

Bryan rolled his eyes. "Nobody talks like the books say. Anyway, I got a B on the spelling test."

"Drinks are on the house. Math?"

Bryan swallowed juice in a hurry. "Hey, I gotta clean up," he declared, and dashed for the stairs in a strategic retreat.

Recognizing evasive action, Savannah winced. "We hate long division."

"Who doesn't?" Jared handed her a bottle of wine. "But a B in spelling's not chump change."

Neither, she thought, was the fancy French label on the bottle. "This is going to humble my spaghetti."

Jared took a deep, appreciative sniff of the air. It was all spice and bubbling red sauce. "I don't think so."

"Well, at least take off that tie." She turned to root out a corkscrew. "It's intimidating. You can—"

He turned her by the shoulders, lowered his head slowly and covered her mouth with his. The top of her head lifted gently away.

"Kiss," she finished on a long breath. "You can sure as hell kiss." After picking up the corkscrew that had clattered to the counter, she opened the wine with the quick, competent moves of a veteran bartender. "Fancy wine and fancy flowers, all in one day. You're going to turn my head."

"That's the idea."

She stretched for the wineglasses on the top shelf. "I'd have thought, after the condensed version of *The Life and Times of Savannah Morningstar,* you'd have gotten the picture that I'm not the wine-and-flowers type."

He brushed a finger over the petals of the roses she'd set in the center of the table. "They seem to suit you."

As he folded his tie into his pocket, loosened the collar of his shirt, she poured the wine. "It was rude of me not to thank you for them. So…" She handed him a glass. "Thanks."

"My pleasure."

"Bryan's going to hide out until he thinks I've forgotten about the math. More fool he. If you're hungry, I can call him down."

"No hurry." Sipping wine, he wandered into the front room. He wanted a better look at the paintings.

The colors were bold, often just on the edge of clashing. The brush strokes struck him as the same— bold sweeps, temperamental lines. The subject matter varied, from still lifes of flowers in full riotous bloom, to portraits of vivid, lived-in faces, to landscapes of gnarled trees, rocky hills and stormy skies.

Not quiet parlor material, he mused. And not something it was easy to look away from. Like the artist, he decided, the work made a full-throttle impression.

"No wonder you turned your nose up at what's hanging in my office," he murmured.

"I've never thought art was supposed to be cool." She moved a shoulder. "But that's just my opinion."

"What's it supposed to be? In your opinion?"

"Alive."

"Then you've certainly succeeded." He turned back to her. "Do you still sell?"

"If the price is right."

"I've been thinking about having Regan do something about my office. My sister-in-law," he reminded her. "She's done an incredible job with the inn she and my brother are rehabing. Would you be willing to handle the art?"

She took it slow, watching him, sipping wine. The idea had an old, deeply buried longing battling for air. Painting was just a hobby, she reminded herself. What else could it be, for a woman with no formal training?

"I've already told you I'd sleep with you."

He managed a laugh, though it nearly stuck in his suddenly dry throat. "Yes, you have. But we're talking about your painting. Are you interested in selling some?"

"You want to put my art in your office?"

"I believe I've established that."

One step at a time, Savannah reminded herself. Don't let him see just how much it would mean. "Wouldn't you be more comfortable with some nice pastels?"

"You have a nasty streak, Savannah. I like it."

She laughed, enjoying him. "Let's see what your sister-in-law comes up with first. Then we'll talk." She walked back into the kitchen to put on water for the pasta.

"Fair enough. Why don't you drop by the inn, see what she and Rafe have done there?"

"I'd love to get a look at the place," she admitted.

"I could drive you over after dinner."

"Homework." She shook her head with real regret. "I have a feeling I'm going to be doing long division."

"In that case—" he picked up the wine and topped off both their glasses "—let me offer a little Dutch courage."

She hadn't expected him to stay after the meal was over. Certainly hadn't been prepared for him to wind things around so that he was sitting beside her son at the kitchen table, poring over the problems in an open arithmetic book.

She served him coffee as he translated the problems into baseball statistics. And why, Savannah wondered, as her son leaped at the ploy and ran with it, hadn't she thought of that?

Because, she admitted, figures terrified her. Schooling terrified her. The knowledge that her son would one day soon go beyond what she had learned was both thrilling and shaming.

Not even Bryan knew about the nights she stayed up late, long after he slept, and studied his books, determined that she would be able to give help whenever he asked her for it.

"So, you divide the total score by the number of times at bat," Jared suggested, adjusting his horn-rims in a way that made Savannah's libido hitch.

"Yeah, yeah!" The lights of knowledge were bursting in Bryan's head. "This is cool." With his tongue caught between his teeth, he wrote the numbers carefully, almost reverently. After all, they were ball players now. "Check this out, Mom."

When she did, laboriously going over the steps of the problem, her smile bloomed. "Good job." She brushed a kiss over Bryan's tousled hair. "Both of you."

"How come I didn't get a kiss?" Jared wanted to know.

She obliged him, chastely enough, but Bryan still made gagging noises. "Man, do you have to do that at the dinner table?"

"Close your eyes," Jared suggested, and kissed Savannah again.

"I'm out of here." Bryan shut his book with a snap.

"Out of here, and into the tub," Savannah finished.

"Aw, come on." He looked beseechingly at Jared.

"Actually," Jared began, "I believe my client is entitled to a short recess."

"Oh, really?" But Savannah's dry comment was drowned out by Bryan's whoop of delight.

"Yeah, a recess. Like an hour's TV."

"With the court's indulgence." Jared shot Bryan a warning look, laid a hand on his shoulder. "What my client means is, thirty minutes of recreational television viewing is appropriate after serving his previous sentence and taking steps toward rehabilitation. After which he will, voluntarily and without incident, accept the court's decision."

Savannah hissed a breath through her teeth. "Lights out at nine-thirty," she muttered.

"All right!" Bryan pumped his fist in the air. "You should have gone for the hour," he told Jared.

"This was your best deal. Trust me, I'm your lawyer."

A grin split Bryan's face. "Cool. Thanks, Mr. MacKade. 'Night, Mom."

"Very fast, fancy talking," Savannah said under her breath as her son dashed upstairs to the little portable in her bedroom.

"I couldn't help myself." Feeling a little sheepish, Jared tucked his hands in his pockets. "He reminded me of what it was like to be a nine-year-old boy and desperate for another hour. Are you going to hold me in contempt?"

She sighed, picked up the empty coffee cups, took them to the sink. "No. It was nice of you to stand up for him. Besides, he'd have wrangled the half hour out of me anyway."

"He deserved it." Jared grinned when she glanced over her shoulder. "So do I. After all, we slogged straight through that math assignment."

"You want thirty minutes of—what was it, recreational television viewing?"

"No." He took his glasses off, slipped them into the pocket of his shirt. "I want you to walk in the woods with me." When her brow creased and she glanced toward the stairs, Jared took her hand. "We won't go far. Hey, Bry!" he called out. "Your mom and I are going for a walk."

"Cool," came the absent, obviously uninterested answer. Jared took her denim jacket from a hook by the kitchen door. "It gets chilly after sundown."

"Just to the woods," she insisted as she shrugged into the jacket. From there, she could hear Bryan if he called her.

"Just to the woods," Jared agreed, and closed his hand over hers. "Do you get lonely out here during the day, by yourself?"

"No. I like being by myself." She walked outside with him, where the air had a faint snap and the sky was so clear the stars almost hurt the eyes. "I like the quiet."

They went down the uneven steps that had been hacked into the bank, then across the narrow lane to where the woods began with shadows.

"I kissed my first girl in here."

The just-greening trees opened to welcome them in. "Did you?"

"Yep. Cousin Joanie."

"Cousin?"

"Third cousin," Jared elaborated. "On my mother's side. She had long golden curls, eyes the color of the sky in June, and my heart. I was eleven."

Comfortable with shadows and starlight, she laughed. "A late bloomer."

"She was twelve."

"So, you liked older women."

"Now that you mention it, that might have been part of the attraction. I lured her into the woods one balmy summer evening, when the sun was going down red behind the mountain and the whippoorwills were starting to call."

"Very romantic."

"It was an epiphany. I drew together all my sweaty courage and kissed her near the first bend in the creek, when the air was full of summer twilight and the smell of honeysuckle."

"That's very sweet."

"It would have been," he mused, "if my brothers hadn't followed us and hidden to watch. They screamed like banshees, Cousin Joanie went tearing back to the farm. Of course, my brothers ragged on me for weeks after, so I had to take on each of them to save my honor. Devin broke my finger, and I lost interest in Cousin Joanie."

"That's sweet, too. The rites of passage."

"I've learned a few things since then, about kissing pretty girls in the woods."

When he turned her into his arms and his mouth

moved over hers, she had to admit he was right. He'd learned quite a number of things.

"Where is cousin Joanie now?"

"In a nice split-level in the 'burbs of Virginia, with three kids and a part-time job selling real estate." With a sigh, he pressed his curved lips to Savannah's brow. "She still has those gold curls and summer eyes."

"One more ghost in the MacKade woods." She looked back through the trees. She could see the lights she'd left on in her cabin. Her son was safe there. "Tell me about the others."

"The two corporals are the most famous. One wore blue, the other gray. During the Battle of Antietam, they were separated from their companies."

He slipped an arm over her shoulders so that they walked companionably, their strides matched. "They came upon each other here, in the woods, two boys barely old enough to shave. In fear, or duty, or maybe both, they attacked each other. Each one was badly wounded, each one crawled off in a different direction. One to the farm."

"Your farm?"

"Hmmm... A Union soldier, torn open by the enemy's bayonet. My great-grandfather, no friend of the

North, found him by the smokehouse. The story is that he saw his own son, who he'd lost at Bull Run, in that dying boy, so he carried him into the house. They did what they could for him, but it was too late. He died the next day and, afraid of reprisals, they buried him in one of the fields, in an unmarked grave."

"So he's lost," Savannah murmured. "And haunts the woods because he can't find his way home."

"That would be close enough."

"And the other corporal?"

"Made it to the Barlow house. A servant took him inside, and the mistress was preparing to tend to him when her husband shot him."

She didn't shudder. She was well used to cruelties, small and large. "Because he didn't see a boy, but the wrong color uniform?"

"That's right. So the mistress of the house, Abigail Barlow, turned from her husband and went into seclusion. She died a couple of years later."

"A sad story. Useless deaths make for uneasy ghosts. Still, it always feels—" she closed her eyes, let the air dance over her face "—inviting here. They just don't want to be forgotten. Do you want to know where they fought?"

Something in her tone had him looking down at her. "Why?"

She opened her eyes again. They were darker than the shadows, more mysterious than the night. "To the west, fifty yards, by a clump of rocks and a burled tree."

He felt cool fingers brush the nape of his neck. But her hands were in his. "Yes. I've sat on the rocks there and heard the bayonets clash."

"So have I. But I wondered who. And why."

"Is that usual for you?" His voice had roughened. Perhaps it was what they spoke of in the night wood. Or perhaps it was her eyes, so dark, so depthless, that he knew any man would blissfully drown in them.

"Your great-grandfather was a farmer who saw a young boy dying and tried to save him. Mine was a shaman who saw visions in the fire and tried to understand them. You still try to save people, don't you, Jared? And I still try to understand the visions."

"Are you—?"

"Psychic?" She laughed quickly, richly. "No. I feel things. We all do. The strongest part of my heritage accepts those feelings, respects them, honors them. I followed my feelings when I left Oklahoma. I knew that I'd find where I belonged. And I took one look at that cabin, at those rocks, these woods, and I knew I was home. I watched you walk across the grass that first time, and I knew I'd end up wanting you."

She leaned forward, touched her lips to his. "And now, I know I have to get back and put my son to bed before he raids the refrigerator."

"Savannah." He caught her hands again before she could turn away. His gaze was intense on her face, almost fierce. "What do you feel about where we're going?"

She felt the heat, then the cold, then the heat once more, slide up her spine. But she kept her voice easy. "I find that when you look too far ahead, you end up tripping over the present. Let's just worry about the now, Jared."

When he lifted her hand to his lips, Savannah realized that now was going to be trouble enough.

She waited until the end of the week before she acted on Jared's suggestion and detoured by the Barlow place. The MacKade place, she corrected, amused at herself for having picked up the town's name for the old stone house on the hill.

The Barlows hadn't lived in it for over fifty years.

The last family, a couple from the north of the county, had bought it, lived in it briefly, then abandoned it twenty years ago. It had been up for sale off and on during those decades, but no one had taken the plunge.

Until Rafe MacKade.

Savannah considered that as she turned off the road and up the steep lane. Someone had begun to clear the overgrowth of brush and brambles, but it was going to be heavy going. Someone, she decided, was going to need a lot of vision.

The house itself was three stories of beautiful stone. Tall windows, arched windows, mullioned windows, gleaming. Most had been boarded up only months before—or so Savannah had been told when she was cornered by Mrs. Metz in the market.

There were double porches. The one that graced the second floor was in the process of being torn down. It needed to be, Savannah mused. It was rotted and sagging and undoubtedly treacherous. But the lower one was obviously new, still unpainted, and straight as a military band on parade day.

Scaffolding ran up the east wing, and piles of material sat under plastic tarps in the overgrown yard. She pulled up beside a pickup that was loaded with debris and shut off her engine.

When she knocked, she heard an answering shout, faintly irritated by the tone of it. She stepped inside and stood, shocked and swamped by the deluge of sensation. Laughter and tears and horror and happiness. The emotions rolled over her, then ebbed, like a breaking wave.

She saw the man at the top of the steps. Smiled, stepped forward. "Jared, I didn't expect to see you. Oh."

She saw her mistake immediately. Not Jared. The eyes were a darker green, the hair slightly longer and definitely less well-groomed. Jared's face was just a bit more narrow, his eyebrows had more of an arch.

But that MacKade grin was identical, as sharp and lethal as an arrow from a master's bow.

"I'm better-looking," Rafe told her as he started down.

"Hard to say. The family resemblance is almost ridiculous." She held out a hand. "You'd be Rafe MacKade."

"Guilty."

"I'm—"

"Savannah Morningstar." He didn't shake her hand, just held it while he gave her a long, practiced once-over. "Regan was dead on," he decided.

"Excuse me?"

"You met my wife last weekend at her shop. She told me to think of Isis. That didn't do me a hell of a lot of good, so she said to think of a woman who'd stop a man's heart at ten paces and have him on his knees at five."

"That's quite an endorsement."

"And dead on," he repeated. "Jared said you might be coming by." He tucked his thumbs in his tool belt.

"I don't want to interrupt your work."

"Please, interrupt my work." He aimed that grin again. "I'm just killing time until Regan gets home from the shop. We're living here temporarily. Want a beer?"

This was the kind of man she understood and was at ease with. "Now that you mention it."

But she hadn't taken two steps behind him when she stopped dead in her tracks and stared at the curve of the staircase.

Intrigued, Rafe watched her. "Problem?"

"There. It was there, on the stairs."

"I take it Jared told you about our ghosts."

She felt weak inside, jittery at the fingertips. "He told me there had been a young Confederate soldier, that Barlow had shot him after a servant had brought him into the house. But he didn't say—he didn't tell me where."

Her legs felt heavy as she walked to the stairs, as she followed the compulsion to go up. The cold was like a blade through the heart, through to the bone. Her knuckles went white on the rail.

"Here." She could barely get the words out. "Here on the stairs. He could smell roses, and hope, and then... He only wanted to go home."

She shook herself, stepped back one step, then two before turning. "I could use that beer."

"Yeah." Rafe let out a long breath. "Me too."

"Do you, ah, do that kind of thing often?" Rafe asked as he popped the tops on two beers in the kitchen.

"No," Savannah told him, very definitely. "There are some places around this area...this house, the woods out there..." She let the words trail off as she looked out the window. "There's a spot on my bank where I planted columbine, and areas of the battlefield that break your heart." With an effort, she shook off the mood and took the beer Rafe offered. "Leftover emotions. The strong ones can last centuries."

"I've had a dream." He'd only told Regan of it, but

it seemed appropriate now. "I'm running through the woods, my battle gray splattered with blood. I only want to go home. I'm ashamed of it, but I'm terrified. Then I see him, the other soldier, the enemy. We stare at each other for a dozen heartbeats, then charge. It's bad, the fight. It's brutal and stupid and useless. After, I come here, crawl here. I think I'm home. When I see her, when she speaks to me and tells me it's going to be all right, I believe her. She's right beside me when someone carries me up the stairs. I can smell her, the roses. Then she shouts, looks at someone coming toward us down the stairs. When I look up, I can see him, and the gun. Then it's over."

Rafe took a long drink. "What stays with me the longest, after it's over, is that I just wanted to go home. I haven't had it in a couple of months."

"Maybe that's because you are home."

"Looks that way." Suddenly he grinned and tapped his bottle against hers. "A hell of an introduction. Are you up to seeing the place, or do you want to pass?"

"No, I'd like to see it. You've done some work in here."

"Yeah." The kitchen had a long way to go, Rafe mused, but the counters had been built and were topped by a warm slate blue that showed off the creamy ivory of new appliances and gleaming glass-fronted cabinets of yellow pine. "Regan put her foot down," he explained. "A workable kitchen and a finished bath and she'd handle living in a construction site for a while."

"Sounds like a practical woman."

"That she is. Come on, I'll give you the tour."

He took her arm and started back down the hallway. "I'd like to start upstairs," she told him before he could open the door to the right.

"Sure." Most people liked to start with the parlor or the library, but he was flexible. As they started up, he felt her hesitate, brace. Just as he felt the hard shudder move through her as they continued. "No one feels it anymore," he said. "Not in weeks."

"Lucky for them," Savannah managed, grateful when they reached the top of the landing. She looked beyond the tarps, the buckets and tools and saw sturdy walls that had been built to last.

"We finished—" He broke off as she turned away from the bedroom he and Regan shared. A room that had belonged to the mistress of the house and had been lovingly repaired, redone and furnished. Saying nothing, he followed her to the opposite wing.

The door had been removed from this room, a room with long windows that faced the outskirts of town. The walls had been painted a deep green, the wide, ornately carved trim a bone white to match the marble of the fireplace.

The floors had been recently sanded. She could smell the wood dust. The little room beyond—the valet's room? she wondered—had been roughed in as a bath.

"The master's room," she murmured.

"We thought it was likely." Fascinated, Rafe watched her walk from door to window, from window to hearth.

Oh, it had been his, Master Barlow's, she was sure of it. He would have studied the town from here and thought his thoughts. He would have taken one of the young maids to bed in here, willing or not, then slept the dreamless sleep of the conscienceless.

"He was a bastard," Savannah said mildly. "Well, he didn't leave much behind." With a smile, she turned back to Rafe. "You're doing a wonderful job."

Rafe rubbed his chin. "Thanks. You're a spooky woman, Savannah."

"Occasionally. I read palms in a carnival for a while. Pretty tedious work, really. This is much more interesting." She moved past him, back into the hall, and headed straight for the mistress's room. "This is beautiful," she murmured.

"We're jazzed about it." From the doorway, Rafe scanned the room himself. He could smell roses, and he could smell Regan. "It's going to be our honeymoon suite."

"It's perfect."

She meant exactly that. In all her travels, she had never seen anything as lovely. Rosebud wallpaper as delicate as a tea garden was trimmed with rose-toned wood. There were beautiful arched windows framed in lace that had the sunlight streaming in patterns on the highly polished floor.

A four-poster with a lacy canopy dominated the space. There were candles, slim tapers of ivory, and rose burned downed to varying lengths that stood on the mantel in crystal holders. An elegant lady's desk was topped by a globe lamp. Petit-point chairs, curved edged tables. A pale pink vase crowded with sunny daffodils.

No, she'd never seen anything so lovely. How could she have? she reminded herself. Her life had been dingy trailers, cramped rooms and highway motels.

Envy snaked through her so quickly she winced.

"Jared said your wife did the decorating."

"For the most part."

What would it be like, Savannah wondered, to have such exquisite taste. To know exactly what should go where?

"It's beautiful," she said again. "When you're ready to open, you'll have to beat off guests with a stick."

"We're shooting for September. It's a little optimistic, but we might pull it off." His head turned, his eyes changed at the sound of the door opening downstairs. "That's Regan."

Savannah had a firsthand view of what a MacKade looked like when he was very much in love. Another surprising snake of envy curled through her.

"Up here, darling," Rafe called out. "I'm in the bedroom with a gorgeous woman."

"That's supposed to surprise me?" Regan strolled into the room. "Hello, Savannah." It was all she managed to get out before Rafe cupped a hand behind her neck and drew her up for a lengthy welcoming kiss. "Hello, Rafe."

"Hi."

They beamed at each other. Savannah could think of no other word for it. Unless the word was *perfect*.

Regan MacKade, with her swing of glossy brown hair, her elegant face with its charming little mole beside the mouth, her lovely blue eyes the color of summer skies, seemed perfect as she slipped an arm around her husband.

Her clothes were beautifully tailored—the teal blazer and pleated slacks, the smart white shirt with the copper bar pin at the collar. She had a sexy-lady scent about her. Not prim, not overt. Just perfect.

Savannah felt like a grubby Amazon who'd stumbled on a princess.

"I've been giving Savannah the tour," Rafe explained.

"Great." Regan pushed back the right curtain of her hair, and rings glittered on her fingers. "What do you think so far?"

"It's wonderful." Savannah remembered the beer in her hand and lifted to it her lips.

"Let's not stop here." With a friendly smile, Regan led the way out. "Jared called the shop this morning and said he'd like us to work on redoing his offices."

"About damn time," Rafe commented. "The place is as cheerful as a mausoleum. White and gray. Might as well work in a tomb."

"We'll fix that." With boundless confidence and en-thusiasm, Regan showed off the house.

Every room, whether it was complete or in progress and filled with nothing more than dust and cobwebs, scraped at Savannah's confidence. She knew nothing of fine antiques, expensive rugs or window treatments.

She didn't want to know.

"Jared's really impressed with your art," Regan went on as they wound their way down to the first floor. "Obviously it inspired him to do something about his work space. I'd love to see some of what you've done."

"It's no big deal. I don't have any training."

Savannah took one long scan of the front parlor, with its curvy settee and elegant side tables, and jammed her hands in the pockets of her jeans. A marble fireplace gleamed like glass, set off with polished brass tools and andirons. And everything, down to the last candlestick, was picture-perfect.

"Nothing of mine would fit in here, that's for sure. Or a lawyer's office, either. Thanks for the tour. And the beer," she added, handing Rafe the empty bottle. "I've got to go pick up my kid."

"Oh." Surprised by the abrupt exit, Regan followed her to the door. "If you've got some time over the weekend, I can fiddle with my schedule. We could work on color schemes and treatments."

"I've got a lot of work." Savannah pulled open the door, suddenly desperate to escape. "You'd better handle it on your own. See you around."

"All right, but—" Regan broke off with a huff when the door closed in her face. She had definitely, and none too subtly, been brushed off. "And what," she asked, turning to Rafe, "was that all about?"

"Don't ask me." Thoughtfully he ran a hand over his wife's glossy hair. "That's a spooky lady, darling. Let's go sit down, and I'll tell you about it."

Chapter 6

When Jared pulled up in front of the cabin, he was puzzled, mildly annoyed, and quite intrigued. It hadn't taken long for word to get to him that Savannah had all but raced out of his brother's house, shrugging off the job Jared had offered her as she fled.

He intended to get an explanation.

Spotting Bryan and Connor in the side yard, he gave a wave. They responded with an answering shout before they went back to the important business of throwing a baseball.

His rap on the door went unanswered, so he walked in without invitation. He doubted he'd have heard one over the screaming rock and roll that shook the cabin. He followed a gut-bursting guitar riff through the kitchen and into an adjoining room.

She was bent over a worktable. The white of the oversize men's undershirt she wore was streaked with paint. Her hair was twisted back in a braid, her jeans were riddled with holes, and her feet were bare.

His mouth watered.

"Hey."

She didn't look up. A look of fierce concentration remained on her face as she worked delicately with a slim brush dipped in brilliant red.

He glanced around the cluttered room. It had probably been intended as a mudroom, as there was a door leading to the outside. Obviously she didn't need or have time for ambience in her work space, he mused.

The light was full and bright through the windows and showed every speck of dust. The floor was aging linoleum decorated with paint spills. Unframed canvases were propped carelessly against the unfinished log walls, steel utility shelves overflowed with bottles and jars, tubes and cans. He could smell turpentine.

And, with relief, he could see the dented portable stereo that was threatening to split his eardrums. He strode over, switched it off, and almost shuddered at the sudden, exquisite silence.

"Keep your hands off my music," Savannah snapped.

"Obviously you didn't hear me come in."

"Obviously, I'm working." She tossed her brush into a jar of solution, chose another. "Take off."

His eyes lit, but he spoke with measured politeness. "Yes, I believe I will have a beer, thanks. Can I get you one?"

"I'm working," she repeated.

"So I see." Ignoring the curse she hurled at him, he leaned over her worktable.

The wicked queen was nearly finished, and her face was terrible in its beauty. Her body was long, elegant, draped in purple and ermine. Her golden crown was as sharp as blades and glittered with wicked-edged jewels. And in her narrow, regal hand, she held a vivid red apple.

"Gorgeous," Jared murmured. "Evil to the bone. Is this from 'Snow White'?"

"No, it's from the Three Stooges. You're in my light."

"Sorry." He shifted slightly, knowing it wasn't what she wanted.

"I can't work with an audience," she said between her teeth.

"I thought you used to paint on street corners."

"This is different."

"Savannah." Patient, he rubbed a slight red smudge from her cheek. "Did Rafe or Regan say something to upset you?"

"Why should they?"

"That's what I'd like to know."

"They were perfectly polite. Perfectly." When he only cocked a brow, she huffed out a breath. "I like your brother, I loved seeing the house. It was fascinating. And your sister-in-law's just adorable."

It was a woman thing, he realized, and took a cautious step back. "You've got a problem with Regan?"

"Who could have a problem with Regan? We just wouldn't work well together. And besides, I don't want my art in your office."

"Oh? Why is that?"

"Because I don't. I had time to think about it, and I decided I'm not interested." She aimed a cool, level look at him. "All the way not interested, Jared. So beat it."

He moved fast. Lawyer suit notwithstanding, she should have expected him to move fast. He had her up from her stool, his hand clamped on her arm, before she could blink.

That didn't mean she couldn't speak.

"I've told you not to grab me unless I ask you to."

"Yeah, you've told me. You've told me a lot of things." For the hell of it, he took a firm hold on her other arm and watched her eyes flame. "Now why don't you tell me what's going on here?"

"I don't have to explain myself to you. You think because I let you kiss me a couple of times, I owe you? I've let plenty of men kiss me, Ace. And I don't owe anyone."

She'd aimed the arrow well. He felt it hit home, stunned by just how sharp the point was. "You owe me the courtesy of an explanation."

"Courtesy doesn't interest me."

"Fine." Then he wouldn't let it stop him. He yanked her close and crushed his mouth to hers in an angry, frustrated kiss.

She didn't struggle. Instinct warned her it would be worse if she struggled. Instead, she kept herself stiff and turned her mind off. Cold rejection, she knew, was more effective than heated protest.

But both her body and her mind betrayed her, and she trembled.

It thrilled him—that quick, involuntary shiver, that low, helpless moan. But temper was still sparking through him when he jerked away.

Her face was flushed, her breath fast. He knew by the look in her eyes that she wanted as he wanted. At the moment, that fact only infuriated him.

"I owed you that," he said tightly. "Now you can tell me again how much you're not interested."

She was interested. Interested in having a man look at her, just once, the way she had seen Rafe look at Regan. And, oh, it was demoralizing to realize she had that vulnerable need inside her.

"In a quick tumble, Jared?" In a deliberately insulting gesture, she brushed her fingers over his cheek. "Sure, baby, when I've got the time."

"Damn it, Savannah."

"You see." She sighed, shook her head. "I knew you'd take it personally. You're the type. And like I said, that's not my type. You're terrific to look at, and you've got a lot of heat. But—" she lifted a hand, tugged on his tie "—just too traditional and by-the-book. Now, Lawyer MacKade, you know all about the laws against trespassing, the sanctity of someone's home. I'm going to ask you real nice, since you like things real nice, to leave. You wouldn't want me to have to call your brother, the big bad sheriff, would you?"

"What the hell has gotten into you?"

"A dose of reality. Now go away, Jared, before I stop asking nice."

He'd be damned if he'd beg. Damned if he'd let her see that she'd wounded him where he'd never expected to be wounded. Iron pride chilled his eyes. He turned and left without a word.

When she heard his car start, and the sound of it going down her lane, she sank back onto her stool and shut her eyes.

She gave Bryan permission for his promised sleepover and enjoyed the noise and bother of two active boys lasting late into the night. She was in the bleachers on Saturday, cheering on her son and his team. And if she looked around now and again, scanning for a tall man with dark hair and green eyes, no one else knew.

At Cassie's insistence, she dropped both boys at Connor's late Saturday afternoon. Home alone, she paced the house, fidgeted in the quiet, and finally went back to work.

The queen was finished, but she still had the prince to sketch. No wimpy, soft-eyed dreamer for her Snow White, Savannah mused as she began running the pencil over the thick white pad. Her Snow White deserved some fire, some passion, some promise of a happy-ever-after with heat.

It was hardly a wonder that her first rough sketch resembled a MacKade. Dragonslayers, she thought with a grim smile. Troublemakers. Who said a prince had to be polite? Hadn't most of them won their thrones in battle first?

Yes, she could see Jared as a fairy tale prince. Her kind of fairy tale. The kind of story that had inspired the legends that had been passed down through the ages, before they became softened and misted to lull children rather than frighten them.

Warrior, avenger, adventurer. Yes, that was the prince she wanted to create.

She began to enjoy herself. The familiar process of bringing something to life through her heart and mind and hand was always fascinating, if not always soothing.

If things had been different, she wouldn't have made

her living from assignments, but from that heart and mind. Painting what she saw, what she felt, what she wanted—for the joy of it.

She was lucky, she reminded herself, to have this much. There had been no art classes in her life, only stolen moments with a pad and colored pencils. Dreams no one had ever understood.

Yes, she was lucky, because her work and the payment for it allowed her to take time for painting, to justify it as a harmless, not terribly expensive hobby.

Quickly, fueled by instinct, she began to add details to the sketch—the diamond-bright dimple at the corner of that sensual mouth, the arrogant arch of an eyebrow, a hint of muscle beneath the cloak, more than a hint of danger in the eyes she would certainly have to paint a grass green.

Hell, she reflected, if nothing else, her brush with Jared MacKade had given her the perfect model for her assignment. The illustration would be a good one. She couldn't have asked for more.

She should never had let herself get caught up in the idea of painting for Jared, or selling him work that she had done for herself.

The sound of a car had her bracing and fighting to squash a little flutter of hope.

But when she went to the door, she saw Regan MacKade. The two women studied each other coolly. After a long moment, Savannah opened the door and stepped back.

"I don't know what's between you and Jared," Regan said without preamble. "And if you think it's none of my business, you're wrong. He's family. But I'd like to know why you've decided you can't stand me to the point where you won't even take a potentially lucrative job just because we'd rub elbows occasionally."

"I don't want the job."

"That's a lie."

Savannah's eyes went molten. "Now look, sister—"

"No, you look." Revved, Regan jabbed a finger at Savannah's chest. "We don't have to be friends. I've got friends. Though I'm baffled at how we could both manage to be friends with someone as sweet as Cassie Dolin. She finds you admirable, and it's not my place to tell her you're just plain rude. You were interested in the job when Jared suggested it. Interested enough to come to the house. And according to Rafe, everything was just dandy until I walked in. Now what's your problem? Sister."

Savannah found her temper warring with amusement, and reluctant admiration. Didn't the woman realize Savannah was big enough to break her in half? "I guess you told me."

"So why don't you tell me?" Regan shot back.

"I don't like the way you look."

"You—I beg your pardon?"

"Or the way you talk." Pleased with herself, Savannah smiled. "Let me guess—private education, dances at the country club, debutante ball."

"I was never a debutante." If she hadn't been so baffled, Regan would have been insulted. "And what's that got to do with anything?"

"You look like you just stepped out of one of those classy women's magazines."

Regan threw up her hands. "That's it?"

"Yeah, that's it."

"Well, you look like one of those statues men sacrificed virgins to. I don't hold it against you. Exactly."

They frowned at each other for a minute. Then Savannah sighed, shrugged. "I've got some ice tea."

"I'd love some."

By the time she was sipping her second glass, Regan

was up and wandering the front room. She stopped by a landscape, all rocky hills and trees gone violent with autumn.

"This one," she decided. "He needs this one where that horrible white-orchid still life is hanging."

"I'd have thought you'd go for the orchids." When Regan turned, her eyes narrowed blandly, Savannah smiled fully for the first time. "Yeah, I can see I'd have been wrong."

"Greens and mauves," Regan announced. "Deep greens. And those chairs in the outer office have got to go. I've got a couple of library chairs in mind. Deep-cushioned, high-backed. Leather. And I figure hard-wood with area rugs, instead of that gray sea of wall-to-wall."

Yes, of course. Savannah could already see it. Regan MacKade was obviously a woman who knew what she wanted. "Look, I'm not a humble person, but can you actually see my paintings jibing with your taste...or Jared's?"

"Yes. And I think, all things considered, that you and I will work together very well." Regan held out a hand, waited. "Well, are we going to give Jared a break and get him out of that tomb?"

"Yeah." Savannah took the pretty hand, with its glittering rings, in hers. "Why the hell not?"

Later, Savannah walked toward the woods. She had to admit she'd done something she detested in others. She had looked at the surface and made a decision. All she had seen—maybe all she'd wanted to see when she looked at Regan MacKade—was elegance, privilege and class.

But who could have guessed there'd be such grit under all that polish?

She should have, Savannah realized.

And when she saw Jared sitting on a rock smoking quietly, she realized she had known she'd find him here.

He said nothing when she sat down beside him and took the cigar. The silence was lovely, filled with birdsong and breezes.

"I owe you an apology." It didn't quite stick in her throat, but she handed him back the cigar. "I was… You caught me at a bad time the other day."

"Did I?"

"Don't make it easy, MacKade."

"I won't."

With a quick, bad-tempered shrug, she swung her

legs up, crossed them under her. "I wasn't completely truthful with you. There are a lot of things I don't mind doing, but lies don't sit well with me. I wanted the job. I can use it. But I felt…intimidated," she muttered as the word sat distastefully on her tongue.

"Intimidated?" It was the last reason or excuse he'd have expected to hear out of her. "By what?"

"Your sister-in-law, to start."

"Regan?" Sheer astonishment ran up hard against the foul mood he'd been mired in for twenty-four hours. "Give me a break."

It was his quick, dismissive laugh that snapped it. Temper soaring, Savannah bolted up from the rock and whirled on him. "I've got a right to be intimidated by whatever I please. I've got a right to feel exactly how I chose to feel. Don't you laugh at me."

"Sorry." Wisely Jared cleared his throat, then looked up at her. "Why would Regan intimidate you?"

"Because she's…she's classy and lovely and smart and successful. She's everything I'm not. I'm comfortable with who I am, what I am, but when you come up against someone like that, it's a kick-in-the-butt reminder of what you're never going to be, never going to have. I don't like feeling inadequate or stupid."

Disgusted with herself, Savannah jammed her hands in her pockets. "And I didn't expect to like her so much. She came by to see me a little while ago."

"I thought she might. Regan likes to confront things head-on." Thoughtful, he studied the tip of his cigar. "Ask her sometime about the night she waltzed into Duff's Tavern in a tight red miniskirt and had Rafe gnawing his pool cue into toothpicks."

Fascinated by the image, Savannah nearly smiled. "I'll have to do that. I'd like to handle the art for your office, Jared, if you're still interested."

"I'm interested." He turned the cigar around, offering it. When she shook her head, he took a last puff and carefully tamped it out on the rock.

"I wasn't completely truthful about a couple of other things." The situation was a first, and she wasn't quite sure how to phrase things, so she decided to keep it simple. "I have feelings for you, Jared. They just sort of popped up. They worried me."

He was watching her now, his wonderful eyes very focused, very cool. She wondered how many witnesses had broken apart on the stand under that strong gaze.

"Men are a lot easier to deal with when feelings aren't involved," she continued. "I could be reading this wrong, but I got the idea you were aiming for a relationship kind of deal, and I've had lousy luck with relationships. So I started thinking about that, and some other things, and figured it was best all around to bail."

When he said nothing—absolutely nothing—she gave in and kicked at the dirt on the path. "Are you just going to sit there?"

"I'm listening," he said mildly.

"Okay, look, I've got a kid to worry about. I can't afford to get involved with someone who might start to mean something to him that's not realistic. I know how to be careful about that, how to keep things in line."

He stood now, his eyes never leaving hers. "You're going to keep me in line, Savannah?"

If he touched her, she was very much afraid she'd go off like a rocket. "I don't think so. That's the thing. I've got these feelings for you."

"That's interesting." He hadn't known she could look so vulnerable. "Because I have these feelings for you."

"You do?" Her hands stayed balled in her pockets. "Well."

"Well," he repeated, and stepped forward. He put his hand on her cheek, and his mouth on hers.

She wasn't used to being kissed this way. As if that

were all—as if she were all—that mattered. It made her weak and woozy. Those tensed fingers went limp. And her heart surrendered.

"Are we straight now?" he murmured.

She nodded and found that feeling of pleasure could be huge, just having a man's shoulder ready to cradle your head. "I hate feeling stupid."

"So you said."

"I don't want to feel stupid about this."

His lips curved as he brushed them over her hair. "Neither do I."

"So we'll make a pact. Whatever happens, neither of us will make the other feel stupid."

"I can agree to that." He lifted her chin for another kiss. "Why don't I walk home with you?"

"All right."

She couldn't help it. She felt stupid and sentimental walking hand in hand with him through the woods, aware of every beam of sunlight, every scent, every sound. She would have sworn that she could hear the leaves growing overhead and the wildflowers struggling toward the sun.

Love, she mused, honed the senses.

"I have to pick up Bryan in a little while." She glanced over. "I can call Cassie and rearrange things."

He knew what she was offering, and could feel the blood humming under his skin. When he brought their joined hands to his lips, he saw the flash of surprised pleasure in her eyes. Not yet, he told himself. Not quite yet.

"We'll both pick him up. What do you say to an early movie, and pizza after?"

She couldn't look at him now, not the way her throat was aching. She knew what he was offering. "I'd say great," she managed. "Thanks."

"Jared's cool." Bryan bounced into the top bunk of his bed, his mind full of scenes from the action flick, his belly stuffed with pepperoni pizza. "I mean, man, he knows everything about baseball, and stuff about the farm and the battlefield. He's even smarter than Connor."

"You're no slouch, Ace." She tousled his hair.

"Jared says everybody's got a special talent."

Interested, Savannah leaned on the edge of the bed so that her face was level with her son's. "He did?"

"Yeah, when we went to get popcorn. He said how

everybody's got something inside that makes him different. He knows on account of he has three brothers and they're a lot alike, but they're different, too. He said I'm a natural."

She grinned. "A natural what?"

"Mom." Rolling his eyes, Bryan sat up in bed. "At baseball. And you know what else he said?"

"No. What else did he say?"

"He said how even if I decided not to be a major-leaguer I could use the stuff I know in other things. Of course, I'm going to be a major-leaguer, but maybe I'd be like a lawyer, too."

"A lawyer?" She felt a little flutter of panic. Her son was falling in love as quickly as she was.

"Yeah, 'cause you get to go to court and argue with people and put criminals in jail. But you have to go to school forever, I mean until you're old. Jared went to college and to law school and everything."

"So can you, if that's what you want."

"Well, I'm going to think about it."

He flopped back down, curled into his pillow in a way that comforted her as much as him. It was the gesture of a child. He was still her little boy.

"Night."

"Good night, Bry." She pressed her lips to his temple and lingered over it a moment or two longer than usual. Long enough to make him squirm sleepily.

She rose, turned off his light, then closed his door, because he liked his privacy.

Her son the lawyer, she thought, and rubbed her hands over her face. With a mother who'd never finished high school.

Then, as the panic gave way to a warm glow of pride for what her son might one day achieve, she smiled.

She walked quietly to her own room and moved to the window to look out at the woods. Through them, she could see the lights of the MacKade farm. And there, she thought, was the man she'd fallen in love with.

She smiled again and laid a hand on the cool glass of the window. All in all, she decided, it had been pretty smart of her to wait to fall until she'd found Jared MacKade.

Chapter 7

He sent her yellow tulips, and she was dreamy-eyed
for an hour after she slipped them, stem by stem, into
numerous old bottles.

He took her and Bryan to a minor-league ball game
in the neighboring county, where the stands were hard
as iron and the crowd was rowdy, and won her son's
heart absolutely by snagging a foul.

They had pizza at a place with worn wooden booths,
a loud jukebox and a pinball machine. The three of
them ate sloppily, shouted over the music and competed
like fiends over the speeding silver balls.

He took her to dinner at a restaurant where there was

candlelight and champagne fizzing in crystal flutes and held her hand on the snowy-white tablecloth.

He brought her a truckload of mulch for her garden, and she was lost.

"You're being courted," Cassie told her over lemonade and paint samples at Savannah's kitchen table.

"What?"

"Courted." Cassie sighed over it. The misery of her years with Joe Dolin hadn't quashed her romantic na ture. Not when it concerned someone else. "Isn't she, Regan?"

"Big-time. Yellow tulips," Regan added, glancing up from her samples to the flowers that marched down the center of the table. "It's a dead giveaway."

"We're developing a relationship." Voice casual, Savannah rubbed her suddenly damp palms on her jeans. "That's all."

"He brought you mulch and helped you spread it, didn't he?" Cassie pointed out reasonably.

"Yeah." It made Savannah smile foolishly to remember it. And to remember the way he'd kissed her senseless when the two of them were grimy with dirt and sweat and chipped bark.

"She's got it bad," Regan commented.

"Maybe I do." Damping the smile, Savannah snatched up her lemonade. "So what?"

"So nothing. What do you think of this shade?"

"Too yellow."

Regan blew out a breath. "You're right."

Filled with admiration, Cassie watched the way her two friends chose and discarded colors. She hoped when she had just a little more put aside, Regan would help her pick out new paint for her living room. She'd washed those white walls so often, scrubbed till her shoulders sang, but she couldn't make them bright again.

Then, if Savannah could help her pick the right material, she could make new curtains for Emma's room. Something cheerful, something special for a little girl.

It was hard, harder than she could admit to anyone, to take on these little challenges. To accomplish things that she imagined were just everyday things to some women. How could she explain that for the first time in her life—her entire life—there was no one to tell her yes or no? No one to complain or criticize or humiliate her?

Constantly she had to remind herself that she was in charge, and that if she tried, if she kept at it step by step, she could change the tiny rented house into a home. A real home, where her kids wouldn't remember the shouting and the beatings and the smell of soured beer.

Wistfully she looked around Savannah's cabin. It was no larger than the house where Cassie lived with her children, but it was so much more. Bright colors, carelessly tossed cushions. Dust.

She still attacked dust like a maniac, afraid Joe would walk in the door and pounce on her for forgetting. No matter how often she told herself he wouldn't, couldn't, because he was locked up, she still lay awake at night, shuddering at every creak.

And woke up every morning relieved. And ashamed.

Her ears pricked. "The kids are coming back," she announced, and pushed all those old fears aside. "Is it all right if I make more lemonade?"

Savannah merely grunted and studied the colors Regan had selected for Jared's law library.

Then the kids burst in like rockets.

"Only three more weeks," Bryan shouted, and waved both fists in triumph. "The kittens can come in three more weeks."

"Happy days," Savannah murmured, but she smiled

when Emma darted over to wrap an arm around Cassie's leg. "Hi, angel face."

"Hello. Bryan let me pet his kittens. They're soft."

"She wants one." Shyness had never been a problem for Bryan. He scooped a hand into the cookie jar and hauled out a fistful. "Can she have one, Mrs. Dolin?"

"What?"

He stuffed a cookie into his mouth and eyed the lemonade Cassie was making. "Can Emma have one of the kittens? Shane's got extra."

"A kitten." Automatically Cassie put a protective hand on Emma's head. "We can't have animals in the house, because—" She broke off, her gaze darting to Connor's, even as her son dropped his head to stare at his feet.

Because Joe doesn't like them. She'd nearly said it, so ingrained was the habit. A habit, she realized, that had prevented her from seeing how longingly Connor spoke of Bryan's expected pets. How much Emma liked to play with the neighbor's little brown dog.

"I don't see why we couldn't."

Her reward was a brilliant and grateful look from her son. "Really?" The disbelief and hope in his voice almost made her weep. "Can we *really?*"

"Sure we can." She scooped Emma into her arms and nuzzled. "You want one of Shane's kittens, Emma?"

"They're soft," Emma said again.

"So are you." It was time she did this, Cassie told herself. Made simple decisions without worrying about what Joe would do. "Tell Shane you'd like one, Connor."

"Cool." Unaware of the drama, Bryan chomped down another cookie. "Then you can bring him over sometimes so he can play with his brothers. Let's go work on your pitching arm, Con."

"Okay." Connor darted after his friend, skidded to a halt. "Thanks, Mama."

"Whoa." At the door, Rafe barely avoided a head-on collision with Connor. He pretended he didn't see the way the boy stiffened and paled, and patted his shoulder, very casually. "You guys are quick. Jared and I lost you in the woods."

"I'm sorry."

"Next year you'll have to try running bases with that speed." He stepped inside, grinned at the ladies. "This was worth a tramp through the woods."

"We're nearly done," Regan told him, and tilted her face up for a kiss.

"No hurry. Hey, gorgeous."

"Hello, handsome." Savannah picked up one of her son's forgotten cookies and offered it.

"Thanks. Cassie—just the woman I want to see."

"Oh? Is something wrong?"

"I've got a problem." To bribe a smile out of Emma, he held out his cookie. "Would you give me a kiss right here for this?" he asked.

Keeping an eye on the cookie, Emma leaned forward and touched her pursed lips to his nose.

"A problem?" Cassie repeated. Nerves humming, she set Emma down and told her to go out and watch the boys play. "What is it?"

"Well, I'll tell you." He leaned back on the counter. "Regan and I found this place a little farther out of town, on the Quarry Road. Needs some work." He grinned at his wife. "We're thinking of moving over in a couple months. Probably around June."

"That's nice."

"Well, the thing is, Cassie, we need somebody at the inn. A—what did you call it, darling?"

"Chatelaine."

"Fancy word for manager, if you ask me. Somebody to look after the place," Rafe explained. "And the guests, once we've got them. Somebody who can cook breakfast, manage the housekeeping. Somebody who wouldn't mind living in and running things."

"Oh." Nerves settled, Cassie smiled. "You want me to ask around. We could put the word out at the diner."

"No, we've already got somebody in mind." Eagle-eyed, Rafe spotted the cookie jar and helped himself. "We want someone we know, someone we trust." He paused to chug down the full glass of lemonade Cassie handed him. "So how about it?"

"How about it?" she repeated.

"That's not the way you offer someone a position, Rafe," Regan said with a sigh. "Cassie, we'd like you to move in and manage the inn for us. We just can't do it, between my shop and Rafe's work."

"You want me?" If she'd still been holding the glass, it would have been smashed on the floor. "I don't know anything about managing an inn. You'd have to have experience, and—"

"You manage a house and two kids," Rafe pointed out. "You cook almost as well as I do. You know how to handle all the customers at Ed's, run the kitchen there when you have to. And you have a soothing personality. Those are qualifications in my book."

"But—"

"You'll want to think about it." Regan's interruption was smooth as silk. "I know it's a big favor, Cassie, and you've worked at Ed's so long that it would be a big decision to switch jobs. But Rafe's fixing up a nice apartment on the third floor—with its own kitchen— that would be part of the salary. You'd have privacy. Maybe you and the kids could come by and take a look. We'd really appreciate it."

An apartment, privacy. No rent payment. That beautiful house on the hill. A manager. It all whirled in Cassie's head like blurred and colorful dreams.

"I'd like to help, but—"

"Great." Flashing a grin at his wife, Rafe patted Cassie's shoulder. "You just come give the place a once-over, and we'll talk about it some more."

"All right." Dazed, she shifted Emma on her hip. "I'll come by. I have to get along. I promised Connor and Bryan we'd have hot dogs on the grill."

"Go on and round them up," Savannah suggested. "I'll run and get Bryan's backpack."

She waited until Cassie was out the screen door. "You make a very good team," she murmured, looking at Regan and Rafe. "And very good friends."

She was nearly at the steps when she saw Devin on

her porch, talking to Cassie. Her back snapped straight. "Something I can do for you, Sheriff?"

Only mildly annoyed at the interruption, he looked through the screen. "No. I just walked over with Jared and Rafe. You've done a nice job on the bank."

"Thanks."

When Emma held out her precious cookie to share, Savannah's brow furrowed. She watched Devin lean forward, take a small bite.

"You taste better," he announced, and made Emma giggle by nuzzling the gentle curve of her neck.

"You can hold me," she told him, tossing out her arms and wrapping them around his neck.

"Thank you, ma'am." He took her, brushing his cheek over her hair before settling her on his hip. As Cassie hurried away to call the boys, Devin looked back through the screen, Emma in his arms. "Some women like me."

Eyes cool, Savannah inclined her head. "So it seems."

"I'm not packing heat, Ms. Morningstar." That lethal MacKade grin flashed, all power and charm. "Just taking in a spring evening with my best girl."

"You're wearing a badge," Savannah pointed out.

"Habit. I've got no problem with you."

"I'm going to keep it that way." She looked across her yard to where Jared was hitting pop-ups for the boys.

"I've got no problem with that," Devin said quietly, and drew her gaze back to his.

"All right." She nodded and headed up to get her son's overnight bag.

Holding Emma, Devin stepped off the porch. He managed to draw Cassie into a brief conversation and charmed one hesitant smile out of her before he had to pass Emma back and watch her and the kids head for their car.

She wasn't quite so thin as she'd been those last months before he was finally able to collar Joe, Devin thought. Though she still looked as though one careless shout would topple her. A man had to be careful with her. The shadows had faded from under her eyes, but the eyes were still haunted.

He worried about her, and wondered. When the car was gone, he tucked his thoughts away and strolled over to Jared. "Your lady doesn't like me."

Jared gave the bat a last swing. "She doesn't like your badge."

"Like I said—she doesn't like me."

Jared looked toward the porch, where Savannah

stood watching them, and felt his heart beat off-rhythm. "She's had a rough road."

"I don't doubt it." He'd seen a few miles of it in her eyes. "She what you want, bro?"

"Looks that way."

"Well, then." Devin rubbed his chin in his thoughtful way, still holding Savannah's cool gaze. It would take a hell of a lot more than a shout to topple that one, he mused. "I have to say your taste in women has improved mightily since your timely divorce."

Surprised, Jared leaned on the bat. "I thought you liked Barbara."

Devin snorted out a laugh. "Yeah, right."

"You never said different."

"You never asked me." Devin picked up the ball from the grass, tossed it high, made a one-handed catch that would have had Bryan cheering. "I like this one."

Bemused, Jared shook his head. "You just said you didn't."

"I said *she* didn't like *me*." Devin's grin was sly and slow. "I find that very attractive in a woman."

Jared had him in a headlock in a blink. Experienced in such matters, Devin overbalanced and sent them both tumbling to the ground.

With the faintest of frowns, Savannah watched them wrestle—much as Bryan and Connor were prone to do. Behind her, Rafe and Regan stepped out of the house.

"Well, hell, they got started without me."

"We're going." Regan took a firm grip on Rafe's arm. "You promised to take me to dinner."

"But, darling…"

"You can fight with them tomorrow. Bye, Savannah."

"Mm-hmm…"

At Rafe's shout, Devin rolled aside and rose, narrowly avoiding the hand that snaked out to trip him. After brushing off his jeans, he jogged down to join Rafe and Regan. He sent one quick salute to Savannah and disappeared into the woods.

"What was that?"

A bit winded, Jared climbed onto the porch. He winced a little and rubbed his ribs. "He got me a couple of good ones."

"Were you playing or fighting?"

"What's the difference?"

She had to laugh. "What were you playing and/or fighting about?"

"You. Got anything cold?"

"Me?" She was in the house behind him like a shot. "What do you mean?"

"He said..." Jared let the words trail off, sighed lustily over the icy beer he'd snagged from the refrigerator, popped it open, then drank deeply. "He said he found you attractive, so I had to pound on him a little."

"Your brother, Sheriff MacKade, finds me attractive."

"Yeah." He leaned over the sink to splash cold water on his face. "He likes you."

"He likes me," Savannah repeated, baffled. "Why?"

"Partly because you don't like him. Dev can be perverse. Partly because I do, and he's loyal." He rubbed his dripping face with a dish towel. "And partly because he's got good instincts and a fair mind."

"Are you trying to make me ashamed?"

"No, I'm telling you about my brother. Rafe's cocky and driven. Shane's good-hearted and laid-back. Devin's fair." Thoughtfully, he laid the towel aside. "I guess it bothers me that you can't see that."

"Old habits die hard." But she could see it, had seen it. "He was sweet with Emma."

Satisfied that he'd found a chink, he grinned. "We've all got a way with the ladies."

"So I've noticed." She took the beer from him and helped herself. "Would you like to stay for dinner?"

"I thought you'd like to go out."

"No." She smiled at the yellow tulips on the table beside him. "I'd like to stay in."

Big Mae, who had run the Tilt-a-Wheel in the carnival where Savannah had worked one educational season, had always said if she ever found a man who could cook and who didn't turn her stomach at the breakfast table, she would give up the high life and settle down.

After being treated to Jared MacKade's Cajun chicken and rice, Savannah thought Big Mae had had a very valid point. She sipped the wine Jared had gotten into the habit of tucking into her refrigerator and studied him over the candles on her dining room table.

"Where'd you learn to cook?"

"At my sainted mother's knee." He grinned. "She made us all learn. And, as she had the most accurate and swift wooden spoon in the county, we learned good."

"Close family."

"Yeah. We were lucky that way. My parents made it easy—*natural* I guess is a better word. Growing up on a farm, everybody has to pull their weight, depend on each other." His eyes changed, and looked, Savannah thought, somewhere else. "I still miss them."

A little jab of envy reminded her that she hadn't known either of her parents well enough to miss. "They did a good job with you. With all of you."

"Some people in town would have said differently once. Some still would." The smile was back in his eyes. "We got our reps the old-fashioned way—we earned them."

"Oh, I've been hearing stories about those bad MacKade brothers." Smiling over the thought, she rested her chin on her fist. "'Swaggering around town' is how Mrs. Metz puts it."

"She would." His smile changed, edged toward the arrogant. "She's crazy about us."

"I thought as much. I was getting the car filled the other day at the Gas and Go when she pulled into the station and got Sharilyn out there by the pumps to reminisce." And, Savannah remembered, to try to pump out a little gossip.

"Oh." Jared cleared his throat. "Sharilyn, huh?"

"Who has some very fond memories of you...and a 1964 Dodge."

To his credit, he didn't wince. "Hell of a car. How's old Sharilyn doing?"

"Oh, she's fine and dandy. Says, 'Hey.'" Amused, she switched gears. "So, which one of you bad MacKade brothers was it who stuffed the potato in the tail pipe of the sheriff's cruiser?"

Jared ran his tongue around his teeth. "Rafe got blamed for it." He lifted his wine. "But I did it. We always figured whatever one of us did, all of us did, so whoever took the heat deserved it."

"Very democratic." She rose to put the dishes in the sink. "I could have used a few siblings on the rodeo circuit. There was never anyone to pass the blame to."

"Your father was rough on you."

"No, not really. He was…" How could she describe Jim Morningstar? "Larger than life, and hard as a brick. He liked a good horse and a bottle of cheap whiskey. He could handle the first, but he didn't do quite so well with the second. He didn't know what to do with me, so he did his best. It just wasn't good enough for either of us."

She leaned back when Jared's hands came to her shoulders as he asked, "Did you learn to ride?"

"So early I don't even remember learning. Could rope

and tie a calf, too. Pulled in a few prizes." She laughed and turned to set her hands comfortably on his hips. "Honey, I learned to do all kinds of wild, wicked things while you were busy steaming up the windows of a '64 Dodge and sticking potatoes in tail pipes."

"Oh, yeah?" He tipped up her chin so they were eye-to-eye.

"Oh, yeah. I could take a horse that looked like two miles of bad road and groom him up till he shined. I liked the ones with temper," she drawled, rubbing her hands up his sides, over his hips. "The ones with fire in their eyes and just a little mean in the heart. I'd make him come to me. Right to me. Then I'd ride him." Eyes open, she scraped her teeth over his bottom lip. "I'd ride him hard and long. And when I was done, he'd be spoiled for anybody else."

His blood went instantly to boil. "Are you trying to seduce me?"

"Somebody's got to." Taking a good, firm grip, she fused her mouth to his until the heat burning through her engulfed him like a flash fire.

His hands gripped like vises on the edge of the sink behind her, his body pressing against hers. And then she was moving against him, sliding, rocking, turning him to iron while her mouth took big, hungry gulps.

"Jared, touch me." Desperate, she yanked his hand free, closed it over her breast, where her heart was pounding like steel on an anvil. "Touch me. Touch me," she repeated, even as his hands streaked under her shirt and filled with her.

She was like some dark, forbidden dream, warm limbs straining against him, sliding, tight denim against tight denim, in painful friction. The flesh in his greedy hands was firm and full and hot. He pressed his mouth to her throat. He could have sunk his teeth into it, such was his sudden, outrageous hunger.

He knew that if he didn't have her now, tonight, he'd be insane by morning.

When he pulled back, dizzy with appetite, she moaned. "For God's sake, are you trying to make me crazy?"

He stared, fighting for his breath as she fought for hers. Though his hands were at his sides now, he could feel her on his fingertips.

"That was the first part of the plan," he said as he took a deep gulp of air, then added, "I'm finished with the first part."

"Hallelujah."

He could almost have laughed. "Bryan's staying at Connor's?"

"Yes." Impatient, edgy, she grabbed his hands. "Come upstairs."

"No."

Her smile was slow and willing. "All right." But when she lifted her arms, happy to take him where they were, he caught her hands.

"No."

"Jared, don't make me hurt you."

He could laugh. "I'm hoping you will. Get a blanket."

"A blanket?"

"I want you in the woods." He turned her hand over in his, caught her wrist in his teeth. "I've always wanted you in the woods."

"I'll get a blanket," she managed, and nearly tripped over her own feet in her rush.

She had herself under control again as they walked together under the arching canopy of trees tender with spring, under the dazzle of stars and the glow of a three-quarter moon. She'd meant to seduce him tonight, to draw him slowly, cleverly in. To surprise him.

She hadn't meant to eat him alive.

Then he stopped where the ground was soft and flipped the blanket down. And she was very much afraid she wouldn't be able to stop herself.

"Tell me something, Lawyer MacKade."

He looked over the blanket at her where she stood, hip shot out, chin angled, eyes full of power and sex. He'd have chewed through glass to get to her. "What's that?"

"Is your health insurance up-to-date?"

His teeth flashed white. "You don't scare me."

"Honey, you won't be able to get your tongue around your own name when I'm finished with you."

She lunged, agile as a trick pony, her legs wrapped around his waist, her hands fisted in his hair. He swung her around once, so that his body would cushion hers when they fell laughing to the blanket.

It knocked the breath out of him, and gave her first advantage.

Her hands were everywhere at once, tugging the shirt over his head, running down his chest to yank at the snap of his jeans. And, to his giddy amazement, her mouth was chasing after them.

"Hold it." In self-defense, he rolled on top of her.

"Keep that up, and this'll last about twenty seconds."
He kept her pinned until his libido could remember it
wasn't sixteen anymore. "I've been saving up for you,
Savannah." He lowered his head, and the kiss was stag-
geringly deep.

The sound she made was a feral purr that shuddered
into his mouth and out the soles of his feet. While his
lips devoured hers, he gave his hands the pleasure of
learning that long, lush body.

Firm and smooth, it moved under his touch sinuously,
inviting him to linger. She smelled like the woods—
dark, mysterious, full of secrets and hidden pleasures.
The taste of that mouth feeding avidly on his was full
of spice and heat.

Her hands were working on his back, tensing his
muscles, nails nipping into his flesh to urge him to
press harder, grip tighter. To take, and take, and take.
Her breath came in low, throaty moans so erotic he
knew he would hear them again in his sleep.

When he reared back, she arched and crossed her
arms over her body. With her eyes on his face, she
pulled her shirt over her head and tossed it aside.

She saw the fresh, wild desire bolt into his eyes, and
reveled in it. In her youth, her body had been a curse—

some had said her downfall. But now, watching the man she loved look at her for the first time, it filled her with a sense of soaring pride.

"It should be illegal." His voice was hoarse and thick. "Looking like you."

He didn't touch her, not yet. Fascinated, he unsnapped her jeans, drew them down and away. His oath was reverent. Then his hands skimmed up, from ankle to knee, to thigh and hip, over the muscled stomach that quivered unexpectedly.

"You're the most terrifyingly beautiful woman I've ever seen."

Her smile was slow, confident. She sat up, hooked an arm around his neck and brought his ready mouth to hers. Her murmur was approving as he explored her, inch by slow, delicious inch. She thought he had wonderful hands, firm, and just rough enough. Her eyes fluttered closed, dreamily, when he used his thumb to torment the tip of her breast.

She could wallow in the lovely feel of flesh sliding on flesh, of the light breeze whispering, the hot blanket beneath. There were owls hooting in the trees, ghosts walking in the air.

Never in her life had she known the magic and the

generosity of love. She knew only that she would give him anything here. Whatever he asked. Whatever he wanted.

When he twisted her hair around his fist, pulled her head back, she was prepared for anything. But he only pressed his lips to her shoulder, rubbed them gently over the curve.

And she trembled like a startled doe.

"Surprised?" Darkly pleased, he lifted his head and looked into her confused, clouded eyes. "You have beautiful shoulders." This time he laved his tongue over them. One by one. Her breath caught on two indrawn gasps. "Sensitive shoulders. They look like they should be carved in marble, but they're soft."

He nipped lightly at her collarbone, and would have sworn it melted. Enthralled with the discovery, he exploited it, lifting her into his lap, so that he cradled her, rather than the ground.

When she was limp. When he knew she was utterly open, he quickly, and with concentrated skill, ripped her ruthlessly to a peak.

She cried out, bucking hard, then pouring into his hand.

Love and pleasure burned through her. Unbearable heat. She turned to him, turned on him, in a wild frenzy of hands and lips. Later, he would think that they had both gone completely mad. But, for the moment, what they did to and for each other was all that made sense.

She made him hiss out her name, and the sound of it sang through her like music. When his heart pounded like thunder under her mouth, she knew it was for her, and only for her. The taste of salty sweat on his skin bewitched her.

He lifted her as though she weighed nothing. She opened, arched, took him deep, so deep that her hands reached out to grip his, from the sheer joy of it. She who cried only when there was no one to see, no one to hear, let the tears fall.

She rocked, matching his rhythm, matching the savage, fearless beat of her own pulse. Endlessly, endlessly, with the stars raining over them and the moonlight slicing through the tender leaves, they took each other.

He was nearly blind from the beauty of her face, electrified from what her body brought to his. He thought he felt something break inside him, around his heart. Then, like some ancient goddess summoning her forces, she lifted her arms high. Gleaming in the stardust, her body went taut, and tightened around him like a velvet fist, and tore him over the edge.

Chapter 8

Savannah awoke with a moan and flung her arm over her eyes to shield them from the blast of sunlight. Her body felt as though she'd ridden a wild bronc over rocky ground.

And then she remembered she'd pretty much done just that.

Her lips curved as the night reeled through her mind. She had thought she knew what it was like to want— a home, a life, a man. She'd been certain she'd experienced every kind of hunger—for food, for shelter, for love. But nothing she had felt before matched what had churned through her for Jared MacKade.

There had been men in her life before—some had passed through, some had stirred her blood. But she had never needed one. And that, she realized, was both the risk and the wonder of this.

There would never be another man. He was the first, and he would be the last, to take her heart.

As both mind and body woke, she heard the song of the birds, the far-off yip of Shane's dogs. She felt the strength of the sun beaming through the spring leaves, and the chill of the early breeze. With her eyes still shielded, she stretched lazily, feeling like a cat waiting to be stroked.

"You have a tattoo."

She made a long, contented sound, flung her arm over her head, and at last opened her eyes.

He was sitting beside her. His hair was tousled from sleep and her hands, his eyes were heavy and focused thoughtfully on an area high on her right thigh. She wondered if there was any other woman in the world lucky enough to wake to such a sight.

"You look good in the morning," she murmured, reaching out to stroke him. "Naked and rumpled."

He wasn't sure how long he'd watched her sleep. But he did know that when he tugged the blanket away from her, to pleasure himself with a long study of her body in the sunlight, he'd discovered the colorful little bird on her thigh.

He simply hadn't been able to get past it.

"You have a tattoo," he repeated.

"I know that." With a little laugh, she rose on her elbows. Those dark-chocolate eyes were heavy and touched with humor. "It's a phoenix," she explained, amused at the way his brows drew together as he focused on it. "You know, rising from the ashes. I got it in New Orleans, when I realized I wasn't going to be poor for the rest of my life."

"A tattoo."

"Some men think they're sexy." Of course, she hadn't gotten it for a man, but for herself. A brand, to remind her that she could remake herself, rise above what she had been. "How about you?"

"I'll have to take it under advisement."

He couldn't say why he was so fascinated by it. So jarred. What other secrets did she have? What other permanent marks from her past? He looked away from it, into her face, and was shaken all over again. The sleepy smile in her eyes, the curve of those lips.

"How're you feeling?"

"Like I spent the night having wild sex in the woods." Laughing, she moved to link her arms around his neck. "I feel wonderful." Her lips found his and lingered, soft and warm. "How about you?"

"Exactly the same."

She hoped so, she hoped he could. She would have lived her life in bliss if he could feel for her even a fraction of what she felt for him.

He gathered her close and held her as no one else had ever held her. As if it mattered.

"I don't suppose we could stay here forever," she murmured.

"No, but we can come back." He needed to think, and knew it was impossible as long as he held her. There were responsibilities at the farm that he was neglecting, he reminded himself. "I have to go." But he buried his face in her hair, and his arms stayed around her. "Farms don't take Sundays off."

"I have to pick up Bryan soon." But her head nestled into his shoulder, and her arms stayed around him.

"Why don't you bring him over and...just bring him over?"

"All right."

"Savannah."

"Hmm?"

He caught her hair in his hand, drew her head back. His mouth crushed desperately over hers. "Just once more," he murmured as he lowered her to the blanket.

When he walked back to the farm, his mind was fogged from her. He'd never known a woman who could leave him so dazed, so weak-kneed. He passed the pigsty, where the stock caught the scent of man and grunted hopefully. In the chicken coop, hens clucked and fluttered over their feed. Distracted, Jared nearly tripped over one of the barn cats, who'd come out to stretch in the sun.

Rubbing a hand over his face, he made it to the back door. The smells of breakfast hit him hard, and his stomach realized it was ravenous. He could have eaten the sausages Devin was grilling, and the skillet along with it.

"Coffee." He nearly whimpered the word as he stumbled to the counter.

Devin glanced at him, then over at Shane, who was already gulping down his second cup. A look of pure enjoyment passed between them.

"Your shirt's inside out," Devin said mildly.

Jared scalded his tongue on the coffee, cursed, then collapsed at the kitchen table.

With a grin cracking his face, Shane leaned on the counter near the stove, where Devin was frying up breakfast. "Brother Jared looks a little rough this morning. Looks like he spent the night crawling through the woods."

"I guess I should have sent out that search party." Enjoying himself, Devin cracked eggs into the pan. "It's tough on a man, spending the night in the haunted woods. Alone."

"I feel real bad about it. Let me get you some more coffee, Jare." All solicitude, Shane brought the pot to the table. "Then you can tell us all about it. Don't leave out a thing. We're here for you."

Jared picked up the coffee Shane had just topped off and scalded his tongue again. "I'm in love with a former exotic dancer with a tattoo."

With an expert's finesse, Devin flipped eggs. "She was a stripper?"

"Where's the tattoo?" Shane wanted to know. It earned him a halfhearted jab in the gut. "Okay, just give me the general area."

"I'm in love with her," Jared repeated, weighing each word.

"Well, hell, you've been in love before." Shane strolled over to take biscuits out of the oven. "At least you've picked one that's interesting this time."

"Shut up," Devin muttered. He heaped food on a platter and came to the table. Then he sat and studied Jared's face. A long moment later, he leaned back and took a considering breath. "All the way in love?"

Experimentally, Jared rubbed the heel of his hand over his breastbone, which ached from the way his heart was swelling. "Feels like it."

With a shake of his head, Shane dumped biscuits into a bowl. "Man, we're dropping like flies. First Rafe, now you." He brought the biscuits to the table, sat, and propped his head on his hands. "It's getting scary."

"Did you tell her?" Devin asked.

"I've got to work it out."

"Next thing you know, we'll have to put on suits again and get married." Grumbling at the thought, Shane started to fill his plate.

"I didn't say anything about *marriage,*" Jared said quickly. Panic reared up and kicked him in the throat. "I've been there. I didn't say anything about marriage."

"You weren't married, you were contracted." Cheering up, Shane shoveled in a man-size mouthful of eggs. A good solid breakfast always lifted his mood. "You might as well have cuddled up with a spreadsheet."

"What the hell do you know about it?"

Shane washed down the eggs with coffee. "Because I never saw you look then the way you look now, bro."

Devin ate slowly and nodded in agreement. "Is it the kid that bothers you?"

"No, Bryan's great." Frowning, Jared helped himself to what was left on the platter. He liked the boy, liked spending time with him, talking with him. And the truth was that one of the reasons his marriage had been doomed was that he'd wanted children, and his wife hadn't.

No, the boy didn't bother him. It was the man who had helped create him who stuck in his craw. And, he realized, the other men since.

He just couldn't intellectualize them away. And he didn't like himself for it.

He caught Devin's look, that quiet, knowing look, and jerked his shoulders restlessly. "I just have to get used to it."

Devin dashed some salt on his eggs. "The trouble

with lawyers is, they like to gather up all the little facts, every little piece. Then they can argue either side. You were always good at that, Jare. Dad used to say you could twist something simple around from right to wrong and back again. Maybe this is one of those times you should just take it as it is."

Jared wanted to. And he hoped he could.

He didn't move in with her, technically. But he spent most of his nights there, and some of his clothes found their way into her closet, his books onto her shelves.

He got into the habit of swinging by after work to pick up Bryan on practice nights. More often than not, they lingered on the field, tossing the ball.

If a case kept him late at the office, he phoned her. Sometimes he phoned her just to hear her voice.

With casual regularity, he brought her flowers, and baseball cards or some other treasure for Bryan. They were a trio on outings, and they gave the town a great deal to buzz about.

Bryan accepted him without question—a fact that both pleased and distressed Jared. He wanted to believe it was because the boy cared for him, considered them a kind of family. But he wondered if Bryan was simply accustomed to having a man stake a claim.

When that nasty toad of a thought jumped into his head, Jared did what he could to bat it away. It was, after all, the now that mattered. The way she looked at him. The way she laughed when she watched him and Bryan tussle on the lawn. The way, he thought, she arched her back after she'd been bending over the flowers she tended, or how complete her concentration was when she worked in her studio.

It was the way she smelled that mattered, when she walked out of a steaming bath. It was the way she strained against him night after night in bed, as if she could never get enough. And the way she would reach for his hand when they sat together on the porch swing in the evening.

Court had kept him late, and the strain of the day refused to be shaken off. He'd brought work home, and he knew that the headache that was drumming behind his eyes would be violent before it was over.

He stopped off in town to pick up aspirin, searching the shelves in the general store for something that promised to kick big holes in the drums in his head.

"Hi there, Jared." Mrs. Metz, armed with a loaf of bread and a box of Ring Dings, cornered him. She was an expert at the ebb and flow of gossip.

"Mrs. Metz." The rhythm of small towns was too ingrained for him to hurry on, and he liked her, had fond memories of her feeding him homemade cookies. And chasing him off with a broom. "How's it going?"

"Fair to middling. Need some rain, that's for sure. Spring's been too dry."

"Shane's a little worried about it."

"We're going to get some tonight," she predicted. "A storm's brewing. Heard that Morningstar boy played a good game Saturday."

"Three RBIs, initiated two double plays."

She gave a cackling laugh that sent her trio of chins waggling. "You sound like a proud daddy." Before he could comment, she hurried on. "Seen you and the boy and his mama here and there. She's what my boy Pete would call a stunner."

"Yes, she is." Jared chose a painkiller at random.

"Hard, though," Mrs. Metz continued, shifting her ample weight to block his retreat. "Raising a boy on her own, I mean. Not that lots of women don't find themselves in that kind of fix today. She's from out west, isn't she? I guess the boy's father's still out there."

"I couldn't say." Because it was the literal truth, the pounding in his head increased.

"You'd think the man would want to see his son now and again, wouldn't you? They've been here close on four months now. You'd think he'd want to come around and visit a fine-looking boy like that."

"You'd think," Jared said, careful now.

"'Course, some men just don't give two hoots, much less a holler, about their children. Like Joe Dolin." Her cheerfully homely face puckered up on the name. "I'm happy as I can be you're handling Cassie's divorce and making it smooth for her. Mostly they're not smooth— I know when my sister's second boy got his, the feathers flew. I'd wager Savannah Morningstar's divorce was a rough go."

Oh, no, you don't, he thought. He wasn't going to give her any fuel by saying there'd never been a divorce, since there'd never been a marriage. "She hasn't mentioned it."

"You used to be more curious, Jared." Before he could snarl at her, she beamed a smile at him. "And just look at you now, a lawyer carrying a briefcase. I've come up to watch you in court a time or two."

His anger with her deflated. "Yes, I know." He'd seen her there, in her large flowered dress and sensible shoes. Like his own personal cheering section.

"Better'n watching Perry Mason, that's what I told Mr. Metz. That Jared MacKade's better'n Perry Mason. Your folks would be right proud of you. And here we thought the lot of you would never be on the right side of the law." She found that so funny, she almost doubled over with laughter. "Lord, you were bad, boy. Don't think I don't know who blackened my Pete's eye after the spring dance in high school."

The memory was very sweet. "He tried to muscle in on my girl."

"Sharilyn got around in those days. It was Sharilyn in high school, wasn't it?"

"Briefly."

"Anyway, she got around, and so did you, as I recall. Girls always fluttering around you and your brothers. Young Bryan's mother must be right pleased to have hooked herself a MacKade, and I got to say, the three of you look real nice together. I got a feeling your mama would've taken to that girl."

"Yeah." Jared felt a clutching in the stomach. What would his mama have said about a woman like Savannah?

He thought about it on the way home, and it added weight to his headache. If his mother were alive, how would he explain Savannah? Unwed mother, exotic dancer, carnival worker, calf roper, street artist.

Pick one, he thought, and rubbed at his temple.

The problem was, he could imagine it all, could see her in each stage of her evolution. And it was too easy to see how each layer was part of the whole that was the woman who was waiting for him.

He was tempted to stop off at Rafe's, or go straight to the farm. Just to prove he could. That Bryan's mama didn't have her hooks in him. But he turned up her lane, because it seemed that anything less would be cowardly.

No MacKade was a coward.

She was playing the music at full volume again. Usually it amused him, the way she would crank up that old stereo and blast rock out over the hills. Now he sat in the car, rubbing his aching head.

He walked to the porch, his heavy briefcase weighing him down. Through the screen door he could see her back in the kitchen, washing dishes, singing along with the stereo in a lusty, throaty voice that would sizzle a man's blood. Her hips were grinding to the beat.

She sure knew how to move, he thought, jealousy and temper slashing through him at the same time the first flash of lightning blazed in the west.

Before he could stop himself, he'd slammed the door behind him. Like a pistol shot, it boomed over the music. She swung around, her loose hair following the flow of her movement.

"You want to turn that damn thing down?" he shouted.

"Sure." Hips still rotating, she sauntered over and flipped it off. "Sorry, didn't hear you drive up."

"You wouldn't have heard a freight train drive up."

She only lifted a brow at the edge in his voice and wiped her damp hands on tight jeans. "Rough day?"

He stalked over, dropped his briefcase on the table where the daisies he'd brought her a few days before still smiled sunnily. "Is that how you danced for money?"

The blow was so quick, so sudden and sharp, she couldn't even gasp. It shivered through her once, viciously, before she gathered herself and rolled over the pain. "No. I wouldn't have made much, if that's all I'd put into it." She walked to the refrigerator for a beer she didn't want, because if there was something in her hands they might not shake. "Want one?"

"No. Didn't it bother you, being stared at, drooled over?"

"Not especially." She look a slow, deliberate swallow of beer.

"So you enjoyed it." He was prodding, very much as he would prod a witness who'd been sworn in. "Enjoyed the dancing, the staring, the drooling."

"It paid the rent. Men liked to look at my body, and I figured they could pay for it."

"And if they'd pay to look, they'd pay to—" He broke off, staggered by what had nearly come out of his mouth. He'd had no idea it was in there.

She didn't so much as flinch. This time, it wasn't unexpected. "Now that you brought it up—" her shoulders moved in a lazy, careless shrug "—I thought about it. There was a time that that was all I had to bargain with, so I thought about selling myself."

The horrified apology that was on the tip of his tongue dried up. "And did you?"

She stared at him, her eyes cool and blank. "I'm going up to say good-night to my son." Her eyes went from cool to ballistic when Jared snagged her arm. "Don't mess with me, MacKade. Stay or go, it's up to you, but don't mess with me."

She jerked free and strode quickly up the stairs.

He wanted to break something. Preferably something sharp that he could stab himself with afterward. Instead, he ripped open the box of aspirin, fought off the lid, then downed three with what was left of her beer.

Upstairs, Savannah settled Bryan in for the night. When she'd closed his door, she locked herself in the bathroom, where she could bathe her hot face over and over again with frigid water.

How stupid she'd been, she thought, berating herself. How blind, not to have seen what he was holding back. How careless, not to have built a defense against what he thought of her, underneath it all.

She would build one now, she promised herself. She would not allow herself to be hurt by the questions he asked, or the ones that were in his eyes. She would not, she swore she would not, allow him to make her feel ashamed of the answers.

She had fought too long and too hard to let anyone make her feel less than what she was.

But, though she tried, she couldn't find that place

inside herself, that quiet, untroubled place where she could escape.

It seemed he could follow her there.

Methodically she dried her face and tidied the sink. All the while, she listened for the sound of his car leaving. But there was nothing but the crack of lightning, the mumble of thunder, and the mutters of old ghosts.

He was at the kitchen table when she came back down, his papers spread out. He slipped his glasses off when she hesitated, but she turned her back on him and walked outside to wait for the storm.

It came slowly from the west, and built. Like temper simmering. The wind kicked up and sent the trees waving. The roar of it—rain, wind, thunder—rolled over the hills, screamed through the woods and exploded.

There was a smell of ozone in the air. A magic smell. A violent smell. Savannah threw her head back and drew it in. When the wind lashed the rain under the shelter of the porch to slap at her face, she stayed where she was. When lightning flashed so close it seemed to singe the trees, she welcomed it.

At length, Jared put his work aside and walked out to her. She was drenched, hair dripping, shirt clinging. The air was cool, but she wasn't shivering. Finally she turned, leaned back against the post and crossed her bare feet at the ankles.

"Something else on your mind?"

He'd taken off his tie and rolled up his sleeves, but he was feeling very much like a lawyer. "The question was crudely put," he began, despising the measured tone of his own voice. "I apologize for that. But not for wanting an answer. I'm asking you if you prostituted."

"That's what's called rephrasing the question. Right, Counselor?"

"I have a right to know."

"Why?"

"Damn it, I'm sleeping with you. I'm all but living with you."

As her stomach clutched and twisted, she angled her head. "Have I charged you anything, Ace?" Her eyes flashed a warning as he stepped toward her. "Don't put your hands on me now. You've got a nerve, MacKade, waltzing in here like it all belonged to you, tossing my past up in my face like you were part of it. Well, it doesn't all belong to you, and you weren't a part of it."

He stepped closer, until he was toe-to-toe with her. The storm flashed and burned in him, around him. "Yes or no."

When she started to shove him aside, he pressed her back, grabbed her chin in his hand. She bared her teeth, and her eyes shot daggers at him.

"You think I want to know? I *have* to know, and I'm prepared to deal with whatever the answer is. Because I'm in love with you." He jerked her chin higher. "I'm in love with you, Savannah."

Her eyes filled, overflowed so quickly his fingers went numb from the shock. She reared back and shoved him with all her strength. "*This* is how you tell me?" she shouted. "Were you a whore, Savannah, I love you? Well, go to hell, Jared. I won't have you cheapening what I feel for you. I hate that you'd make me feel cheap when I hear it, when I tell you what I wasn't sure you wanted to hear from me. I love you so much I'd settle for anything you gave me. Even this."

"Don't." He had to stop himself from springing forward when she reached for the door. He couldn't touch her now, knew he didn't deserve to. "Please don't walk away. You're right. You're exactly right."

She stared through the screen at the home she'd fought all of her life to make. She closed her eyes and thought of the man behind her, a man she'd never have believed she could have.

Suddenly she was exhausted, beaten by her own heart. "I never sold myself," she said quietly, in a voice carefully picked free of emotion. "Not even when I had to go hungry. I could have, there were plenty of opportunities, and plenty of people who assumed I did. But I didn't. I didn't make the choice for myself. I made it for Bryan, because he didn't deserve a mother who would sell herself for food or a night's rent."

She drew in a deep breath before she turned. "Does that satisfy you, Jared?"

He would have taken it all back if he could. Yet he knew that if it hadn't come out, it would have festered and poisoned everything they had. Just as he knew that there was still more that had to be said, had to be asked. But not tonight.

"Can you understand that I hate knowing you had to make the choice? That you were alone, and in trouble?"

"I can't change anything about the last ten years, and I wouldn't."

He stepped toward her slowly, testing. "Can you understand that I love you? That I've just come to realize I've never loved a woman before, and this terrible need I have for you is making me crazy?" He lifted a hand, touched just the tips of her wet hair. "Let me hold you, Savannah. Just hold you."

He took her gently, closed her in his arms and rocked. Relief coursed through him when her arms finally came up from her sides and circled him.

"I hurt you. I'm sorry. I didn't even know I could." Ashamed, he pressed his lips to her hair. "I thought it was all me. It's gotten so huge I didn't think anybody else could feel like this. Let me plead insanity."

"It doesn't matter." She thought she would have crawled inside him if she could. "It doesn't matter now."

"Let me tell you again." Gently he tipped her head back, looked into those dark, damp eyes. "I love you, Savannah. I'm so desperately in love with you." He touched his lips to hers, felt the tremor. "So helplessly in love with you. It takes my breath away every time I see you."

She couldn't speak. This was how she had once dreamed he would look at her, with violent love in his eyes. These were words she'd refused to let herself dream of hearing. She threw her arms around his neck and clung for her life.

"You're trembling," he murmured. "You're cold."

"No. No. Oh, I love you. I don't know how else to say it."

"That'll do. Storm's passing." He could hear the thunder rolling away. "We're going to have a good farmer's rain. A soaker. The kind that means something." He hooked an arm under her knees, lifted her. "I want to make love with you and listen to the rain."

He was so gentle, it seared her heart. Kissing her cheek, her throat, as he carried her to the room they shared. When the door was closed, he walked through the shadows and laid her down.

She heard the hiss of a match, then candlelight flickered. He peeled off her damp clothes, stroked his hand over her skin. And suddenly she felt fragile and nervous.

She knelt on the bed to unbutton his shirt, and her fingers were clumsy. He took them, pressed them one by one to his lips.

There was the smell of rain and wet earth, the whisper of thunder moving off, the give of the mattress beneath her.

Then there was only him. Murmurs and sighs drifted through the sound of pattering rain. He was so tender with her, so gentle, her body seemed to flow through his hands like fragrant heated wax. Each time their lips met, it was deeper and truer. Each time their bodies pressed, it was softer and warmer.

A brush of fingertips, the trail of quiet kisses, and flesh quivered. Dazed with love, they watched each other, listened to the quickening rhythm of hearts.

He slid into her silkily, his sigh merging with hers, his body rising and falling with hers. His lips meeting hers.

He felt her crest sweep through him, a long, slow, undulating wave that carried him off in its wake.

Chapter 9

Bryan loved spending time on the farm. The animals, the men, the open air. He still remembered the confusion and confinement of cities—the places where they had moved and lived in small rooms where the windows always seemed to pulse with noise and the walls were so thin you could hear every laugh or curse from the people next door.

He hadn't minded the city, really. There had always been something to do, somewhere to go. And his mother had taken him to parks and playgrounds—whenever she wasn't working.

He had vague memories of times when she had

worked late into the night, or late into the morning. Times when she'd been tired a lot, and sad, too. Though he hadn't really understood why.

He remembered New Orleans, with the pulsing music and the slow-talking people. He remembered his mother had kept a pot of red flowers on the windowsill.

Sometimes he'd sat at his mother's feet, playing cars or reading picture books while she painted things, painted people who'd come by to sit in a little folding chair while she sketched their faces on big sheets of paper with charcoal or colored chalk.

That was when things had changed. Things had gotten better. She'd stopped working at night, and that sad, tired look had left her eyes.

Now, this was best of all. Having a house, the way she'd always promised. Having a yard and friends who could stay your friends because you were staying, too. Friends like Connor. Who was definitely cool, even though some of the kids at school teased him and said rotten things about his old man.

Maybe, Bryan sometimes thought, it was because they didn't know what it was like to have no father at all. The way he did.

But Mom was enough. She always made things work

out, always made sure they were a team. As moms went, he figured, she was the coolest.

Like the way she'd asked him if he wanted to live in the cabin in the woods. She hadn't just told him they would live there, the way he knew some parents did things. Then, when they had the cabin—which was in his opinion the best place in the whole world—she'd let him pick out the stuff for his room. The neat bunk beds, the posters for the walls, the big wood chest for his toys.

Now he got to visit the farm whenever he wanted. Mostly.

Shane was great. He never minded if Bryan wanted to hang out and ask questions about things. Devin was okay, too, even if he was the sheriff. He liked Rafe, and the way Rafe would sometimes plunk himself down and wrestle with the dogs.

Jared was kind of scary, because he made Bryan think about how it would be to have him around all the time. Like a father. A guy to play ball with. A man who came home after work every day and listened to what you wanted to say. A man who kissed your mother in the kitchen like it was no big deal.

He wanted Jared most of all, and because he did,

Bryan wished for him hard, every night. Somehow, whatever he wished for hard almost always came true.

On the farm, the sun was bright, warming ground that was damp from the night's rain. The early-morning fog had burned off and left the air clear and moist. He was happy sitting on the dirt with the dogs and Connor, with the sound of adult voices never far off. They were going to have Sunday dinner at the MacKades'.

The men were cooking, which Bryan thought was a little weird, but interesting.

"Do you think Fred and Ethel'll have babies?"

Connor continued to stroke the golden fur of the dog nearest him as he considered the question. "They probably will. That's what happens when people are married. It's the same for dogs, I guess."

Bryan gave a snort and delivered a punch to Connor's shoulder. "People don't have to be married to have a kid. They just have to be stuck on each other."

If anyone else had made the comment, Connor would have flushed. But because it was Bryan, he only nodded wisely. "Then Fred and Ethel can have pups, because they're stuck on each other."

Bryan looked toward the farmhouse. Through the

kitchen window came the sound of mixed laughter. "I think Jared's stuck on my mom."

Connor's pale gray eyes went wide. "Are they having a baby?"

"No." Bryan hooked an arm around Ethel's neck. It was a possibility he'd given some thought to. "It'd be cool if they did. I mean, you like having Emma around, don't you?"

"Sure."

"A brother would be neater, but even a sister would be okay. I think if there was one—you know, a baby— Jared would hang around. Like live with us."

"Sometimes it's bad," Connor said quietly. "Sometimes when a man lives with you, it's bad. They argue and fight, and they get drunk and...things."

The idea of that had Bryan's brow furrowing. "But not all of them."

"I guess not." But Connor was far from sure. "I don't want a man to live with us ever again." Connor's voice was low and fierce. "Not ever again."

Understanding, Bryan shifted his arm from Ethel's neck to Connor's. "If your father tries to come back after he gets out of jail, you'll be ready. We'll be ready," he added with a dazzling smile. "You and me, Con."

"Yeah." Connor almost wished he had a chance to prove it. "You and me."

"Looks like they're talking big talk," Savannah commented from the kitchen window.

"Connor's never really had a close friend before." Hadn't been able to, Cassie thought, with the way Joe hassled everyone who came to the house.

"Neither has Bry. They're good for each other." She grinned when the boys started wrestling each other, and the dogs. All four would be filthy, she was sure, by the time dinner was ready.

"That looks familiar." Devin stepped up behind the women, tucked his hands in the back pockets of his jeans. Savannah did her best not to stiffen. "We spent a lot of Sunday afternoons kicking up dirt."

"We spent a lot of every afternoon kicking up dirt," Rafe said.

"Remember that Sunday Mom turned the hose on us?" With a sigh, Shane popped a radish into his mouth. "Those were the days. She was so ticked because Gran and Pop were coming to dinner, and we'd gotten into a fight wearing our best clothes."

"You started it," Jared remembered. "Swiped my baseball and lost it in the cornfield."

"I borrowed your baseball," Shane told him. "And Devin lost it in the field."

"Rafe lost it," Devin said mildly. "He was supposed to catch it."

"You hit it wide. Pulled it," Rafe explained in disgust. "He could never pick his spot."

"Hell I couldn't."

Before Devin could take the argument any further, Regan held up her hands. "Time-out. I believe, with this obvious example of family solidarity, it's an excellent time to make an announcement." She smiled at Rafe. "Don't you think?"

"I think." Rafe took her hand, brought it to his lips before pulling her close. His grin was quick as lightning. "We're having a baby."

There was a moment of utter silence before the explosion. There was a quick whoop from Shane, who took it upon himself to scoop Regan off her feet. She had to be kissed, Rafe had to be punched and pummeled.

"Give me my wife," Rafe demanded.

"In a minute." Shane kissed her again, heartily, then started to pass her to Rafe. Jared intercepted, gave her a quick swing. Regan was still laughing when she found herself in Devin's arms.

"Damn it, give me my woman."

As they tussled and argued over the expectant mother, Savannah leaned back against the counter. "The MacKades—the next generation," she murmured to Cassie. "Scary thought."

"She'll handle it." Cassie blinked back tears. "She can handle anything."

Because everyone else was busy, she scooted over to check on the pot roast herself.

Savannah stepped forward, leaned in to kiss Jared on the cheek. "Congratulations, Uncle Jare."

He couldn't stop grinning. "Rafe's going to be a daddy."

With one brow arched, Savannah glanced over to where Regan was still being passed from brother to brother. "And this, I take it, is the way you guys celebrate—tossing women around."

"We don't have a precedent. It's our first baby."

When he swung an arm around her shoulders, Savannah realized he'd just said it all. It would be a MacKade baby, and would belong to all of them.

It was something she thought about quite a bit as the

celebration continued through dinner with constant, and often ridiculous, suggestions for child care, baby names and fatherly duties. It was odd for her to fully realize now, when she was finally settled into a home of her own, finally confident that Bryan had the best she could give him, that neither of them had ever known the fullness of family.

They had each other, and that was important. Vital. He was a happy, well-adjusted child. She could see that as he sat beside her, shoveling in food, giggling at Shane's idea of Lulubelle MacKade if the baby was a girl. There was no doubt in her heart that her son was exactly as he should be.

And yet.

He had never known the joy, or the problems, of having uncles, aunts, grandparents. Siblings. Those were things she couldn't give him. She hoped it was only she who had suddenly come to sense the lack.

"Are you feeling all right, Regan?" Cassie's voice was quiet amid the chaos of male-dominated conversation.

"Wonderful. I don't think I've ever felt better. No queasiness, no fatigue, not any of the things the books warn us about."

"I had them all." Running an absent hand over

Emma's curls, Cassie smiled. "Not too bad, really, just enough so that when it came around the second time I knew what to expect. How about you, Savannah?"

"Sick as a dog for three months." Before Bryan could reach over her plate, she passed him the bowl of roast potatoes he'd aimed for. "It was almost worth it, though." She winked at Bryan.

"Three months?" Regan gave a heartfelt shudder. "Every day?"

"Rain or shine," Savannah said cheerfully. "Bry, if you opened your mouth just a little wider, you could probably fit three potatoes in at once."

He managed a sloppy grin with a full mouth. "It's good."

"Just like Mom used to make," Devin put in, and heaped another helping of potatoes on Bryan's plate. "We used to have contests to see who could eat more of them. Jared usually won—right, Jare?"

"Yeah." But he'd stopped eating, and he was looking at Savannah oddly.

"The kid's going to break your record." Shane tossed a biscuit that Jared was just quick enough to catch.

Intrigued with the maneuver, Bryan snatched one and aimed it at Connor, who nabbed it before it hit the floor.

"Good save," Rafe commented. "Sign him up. You gonna play ball next year, Con?"

"I don't know." Connor broke off an end of the biscuit and shot a look at his mother under his lashes.

"Con's a better pitcher than any of our starters." Bryan cheerfully helped himself to another biscuit and buttered it lavishly. "He can drill it right in the pocket."

"Connor, you never said you wanted to play ball." The moment the words were out of Cassie's mouth, she regretted them. Of course he'd said nothing. There had never been anyone to play ball with him. And his academic achievements had equaled failure as a man, in his father's opinion.

"I can't hit hardly anything," Connor mumbled, reddening. "I can just throw a little since Bryan's been showing me how."

"We'll have to work on your batting." Devin spoke casually. "After dinner, we could start on your stance."

Connor's lips fluttered into a smile, and that was answer enough.

A short time later, the sounds of shouts and arguments rolled in from the barnyard and into the kitchen window. With her hands filled with dishes, Cassie looked out. Devin was crouched behind Connor, and their hands were meshed on a wooden bat as Jared threw underhand pitches.

"It's awfully nice of them to play with the kids like this."

"And leave us stuck with the dishes," Savannah pointed out.

"He who cooks doesn't clean." Regan filled the sink with hot water. "MacKade rules."

"It's fair enough," Savannah allowed. But as she glanced around the cluttered, disordered kitchen, with its piles of pots and mountains of dishes, she wasn't sure who'd come out on top of the deal.

"Do you mind if I ask..." Regan caught herself, laughed nervously. "It's stupid."

Savannah grabbed a dishcloth and prepared to dig in. "What?"

"Well." Brows knit, Regan attacked the first plates. "I was just wondering, since you've both been through it, what it's like. The big guns, I mean."

Savannah glanced at Cassie and grinned wickedly. "Labor and delivery, or a march through the Valley of Death."

"Oh, it's not that bad. Don't scare her." Immediately

solicitous, Cassie set down stacked plates to rub Regan's shoulder. "Really it's not."

"You want to tell her it's a walk on the beach?" Savannah asked. "Then she can curse you and Rafe during transition."

"It's a natural part of life," Cassie insisted, then struggled with a chuckle. "That hurts like hell."

"Sorry I asked." But Regan blew out a breath when she realized she couldn't let it go. "So, how long did it take?"

"For Connor, just over twelve hours, for Emma less than ten."

"In other words," Savanna put in helpfully, "the rest of your life."

"I'd tell you to shut up, but I want to know how long it took you." Regan wrinkled her nose. "Ten minutes, right?"

Savannah picked up a dish. "Thirty-two fun-filled hours."

"Thirty-two?" Stunned, Regan nearly bobbled a wet plate. "That's inhuman."

"The luck of the draw," Savannah said lightly. "And the maternity ward I was in wasn't exactly first-class. Wouldn't have mattered." She shrugged it off.

"Babies come when they come. You'll get through it fine, Regan. Rafe'll be right there. And unless your doctor has a line of pro-football blockers holding them off, the rest of the MacKades will be there, too."

"You were alone," Regan murmured.

"That's the way it shook down." She glanced over when she spotted Jared at the screen door. "Game over?"

"No." His eyes stayed on hers, unreadable and deep. "I lost the draw to fetch beer."

"I'll get it." Cassie was already hurrying to the fridge. "Do the kids want anything?"

"Whatever they can get." He took the six-pack and boxes of juice Cassie handed him, then left without another word.

"No quicker way to get rid of a man than for women to talk about childbirth." Savannah's voice was light, but there was a knot of worry at the back of her neck. Something had been in those eyes, she thought, that he hadn't wanted her to see.

"I mentioned Lamaze classes to Rafe, and he went dead white." Amused, Regan slipped another dish in the drainer. "But then he gritted his teeth."

"He'll do fine." With a last glance at the screen door,

Savannah picked up another plate. "He loves you. That's the big one, isn't it?"

"Yeah." With a dreamy little sigh, Regan plunged into the dishwater again. "That's the big one."

On the walk home, Savannah spied her first firefly glinting in the woods. Summer was coming, she thought, watching Bryan dart ahead, charging invisible foes. She wanted it to come. She wanted the heat, the long, hazy days, the close, airless nights.

What she wanted, Savannah realized, was the passing of time. A full year, four full seasons, in this place. In this home. With this man.

"Something's on your mind?" she said quietly.

"I've got a lot on my mind." Jared wished they could stay in the woods for a time. Stay where they could both feel the sorrows and needs of people who had died before either of them were born. "Couple of cases driving me crazy. Painters cluttering up the office. Finalizing Cassie's divorce. Contemplating becoming an uncle."

"You're being a lawyer, MacKade, using words to cloud the basics."

"I am a lawyer."

"Okay, let's start there. Hold on a minute. Bry, hit the tub," she called out.

"Aw, Mom..."

"And hit it hard, Ace. I'm right behind you."

He raced ahead, and from the edge of the woods Savannah watched the lights switch on one by one as Bryan streaked through the house. Through the open window, she could hear him singing, miserably off-key, and was satisfied that he was in his bathtime mode.

"Why are you a lawyer?"

The question stumped him, mainly because his mind was so far removed from it. "Why am I a lawyer?"

"And try to answer in twenty thousand words or less."

"Because I like it." The first answer was the simplest. "I like figuring out the best arguments, wading through and studying both sides until I find the right arguments. I like winning." He moved his shoulders. "And because justice is important. The system of justice, however flawed, is vital. We're nothing without it."

"So, you believe in justice, and you like to argue and win." She tilted her head at him. "Which puts all of that into one sentence. See how easy it is?"

"What's your point?"

"My point is that you also like to complicate things." She touched a hand to his cheek. "What are you complicating now, Jared?"

"Nothing." Because he needed to, he took her wrist and pressed his lips into her palm. "I'm not complicating a thing. I liked having you at the farm, you and Bryan. Crowded around the kitchen table, with too many people talking at once."

"And throwing biscuits."

"And throwing biscuits. I liked hearing you and Regan and Cassie clattering around the kitchen while we were playing ball outside."

"Typical." She smiled a little. "You'd say traditional male-female placement."

"Sue me." He gathered her close. And there, in the quiet, he thought he could hear the struggle. Stranger against stranger, hand to hand, eternally. Right, perhaps, against right. "Feel it?" he murmured.

"Yes." Fear, she thought, closing her eyes. Desperation. And constant bleeding hope. Perhaps she could feel the echoes of it in the woods because she'd known all those emotions so well. "Have you ever asked yourself why they're still here? What they might have left to say or do?"

"The fight's not over. It never is."

She shook her head. "The *need's* not over. The need to find home. To find peace, I suppose. It never is. But I'm finding it here."

When she started to draw back, he tightened his grip. "I listened outside the door to the three of you talking in the kitchen. It bothered me, Savannah, hearing about you being alone when you had Bryan. It bothered me imagining that, the way it bothered me when you said you'd been sick all that time."

"Morning sickness is pretty common among pregnant women."

"Being sixteen, alone, sick and pregnant isn't common. It sure as hell shouldn't be."

"Feeling sorry for me is a waste of time. It was a long time ago." Now she did draw back, and she saw his face. "But that's not exactly what you're feeling."

"I don't know what I'm feeling." Nothing frustrated him more than not being able to see inside himself for the answers. "I've got questions I haven't figured out yet how to ask. You make me ask, because you don't tell. And yes, I do feel sorry for you, for the kid who was left to fend for herself, and make choices for herself that no child should have to make."

"I wasn't a child." Her voice was measured, her shoulders were suddenly stiff. "I was old enough to get pregnant, so I was old enough to face the consequences. And the choice I made was mine alone. No one else could have made it for me. Having Bryan was one of the few right decisions I made."

"I didn't mean that. I didn't mean Bryan." Seeing the heat in her eyes, he gave her a quick shake. "I meant where to go, what to do, how to live. God, how to eat. And, damn it, Savannah, you *were* a child. You deserved better than what you got."

"I got Bryan," she said simply. "I got better than I deserved."

He couldn't make her see what he wanted her to see. For once, he simply didn't have the words. Perhaps they were too simple. "I wonder what it would be like to create something like that boy, and to love without restriction. Without ego."

She could smile now. "Wonderful. Just wonderful. Are you coming home with me?"

"Yeah." He took her hand. "I'm coming home with you."

He thought about that kind of love, and her kind of life, as she slept beside him. He would never have gone out and searched for a woman like her. It bothered him a great deal to admit it, even to himself.

She wasn't polished, or cultured, had no sheen of the sophistication he usually looked for in a woman.

That he *had* looked for, Jared reminded himself, once. And that had certainly been a pathetic mistake. And yet didn't a man need a woman he understood, a woman he knew? There were huge pockets in Savannah's life he neither understood nor knew. Large pieces of her that were separate from him, tucked away in her memories.

A young girl, pregnant and alone, deserted by everyone she should have been able to count on. He felt pity for that girl, as well as—and it scalded him to realize it—a vague distrust.

Where had she gone, what had she done, who had she been? As much as he wanted to get beyond that, his pride held him fast. She'd borne another man's child, been other men's fantasies.

That thought stuck in the pride, in the ego, and refused to be shaken free.

His problem. He knew it, rationalized it, debated it. As she shifted beside him, turning away rather than towards him, he worried over it.

How many other men had she loved? How many had lain beside her, each wishing he was the only one?

Yet, even as he thought it, he reached out to hold, to

possess her. Her body curled warm against his, and he could smell her skin, that earthy, sensual fragrance she carried without the aid of perfumes.

He knew her routine now. In the morning she would wake early, but slowly, as if sleep were something to be eased out of, like a warm bath. She would touch him, long strokes over the shoulders, the back, the arms. And just when he began to tingle and heat, she would rise out of bed. She would arch her back with a lazy, feline movement. Lift that long, thick black hair up, let it fall.

Then, as if there were no difference between a sleepy siren and a sleepy mother, she would slip into a faded blue cotton robe and go out to wake Bryan for school.

And often, very often, Jared would lie in bed for long, long moments after she padded across the hall. Aching.

He almost wanted to believe she'd woven some sort of spell over him with her gypsy eyes and sultry smile and that go-to-hell-and-back-again attitude. She knew him better than he knew her. Knew his ghosts, recognized them, felt them. She was the first woman who had walked in what he considered his woods and heard the murmurs of the doomed.

It linked her with him in a way that went beyond the

physical, even the emotional, attraction. It lifted it into the spiritual. It lifted it beyond what he could fight, even if he wanted to fight.

Whatever it was that bound him to her gave him no choice but to keep moving on the same path toward her.

So he fell asleep with his arm hooked around her waist, holding her close. And dropped weightlessly into dreams.

There was pain in his hip where a mortar blast had sent him flying into the air, and hurled him down again. His head was aching, his eyes were tearing. It was so hard to focus, hard to force himself to set one foot in front of the other.

He didn't remember entering the woods. Had he crawled to the trees or run into them? All he knew was that he was terribly lost, and terribly afraid. His lieutenant was dead. There were so many dead. The boy from Connecticut with whom he'd shared last night's dinner, with whom he'd whispered long after the fires burned out, was in pieces in a shallow ditch where the fighting had been so fierce that hell would have been a relief.

Now he was alone. He knew he had to find somewhere to rest, someplace safe. Just for a while. Just for a little while. His home wasn't so very far away. Just north into Pennsylvania. The Maryland woods weren't so very different from those near his farm.

Maybe he could be safe here until he could find his way home again. Until this war that was supposed to have been an adventure and had become a thousand nightmares was over.

He had turned seventeen the month before, and he had never tasted a woman's lips.

Unbearably weary, he stopped to lean against a tree, drew in ragged breath after ragged breath. How could the woods be so beautiful, so full of color and the smells of autumn? How could that horrible noise keep going? Why wouldn't the guns stop blasting, the men stop screaming?

When were they going to let him go home?

With a shuddering sigh, he pushed off the tree. He skirted a rock and, with a burst of relief, spotted a path. Just as he stepped toward it, he saw the Confederate gray.

He hesitated only a moment, but whole worlds revolved inside him. This was the enemy. This was death. This was the obstacle in the path leading to what he wanted most.

He shouldered his rifle even as the boy facing him mirrored the movement.

They shot poorly, both of them, but he heard the whine of the shell close enough to his ear to stop his heart for a full beat. Then he was charging, even as his mirror image charged.

Their terrified war cries echoed each other. Bayonets clashed.

The enemy's eyes were blue, like the sky. That thought intruded as he felt the first agony of blade in flesh. The enemy's eyes were young and full of fear.

They fought each other like wild dogs. Even in the short time he had left, he would remember little of it. He remembered the smell of his own blood, the feel of it as it poured out of his wounds. He remembered waking alone, alone in those beautiful autumn woods.

And then stumbling down the path. Crawling, crying.

He would remember, for all of the hours he had left, he would remember the sight of the farmhouse just beyond the clearing. The color and glint of the stone, the slope of the roofline, the smell of animals and growing things.

And he wept again, for home.

Someone was with him. The face was older, weathered, set in a frown under a soft-brimmed hat. He thought of his father, tried to speak, but the pain as he was lifted was worse than death.

There were women around him, shouts, then whispers. Soft hands and firelight. Cool cloths, and the pain slipped into numbness.

Every word he spoke was a searing flame in his throat. But he had so much to say. And someone listened. Someone who smelled like lilacs and held his hand.

He needed to tell her he'd been proud to be a soldier, proud to serve and to fight. He was trying to be proud to die, even though the longing for home was fiercer than any of his wounds.

When he died, Jared woke, his heart stuttering. Savannah stirred beside him. And this time, this time, turned to him. In sleep, her arms came around him.

For tonight, it was enough.

Chapter 10

With a stack of three paintings balanced in her arms, Savannah muscled open the door to Jared's offices. Rain dripped from the bill of one of Bryan's baseball caps, which she'd slapped on before making the drive to Hagerstown. Sissy glanced over, then hopped up from her keyboard.

"Let me give you a hand with those."

"Thanks." Grateful, Savannah passed the three wrapped bundles over. "I've got more in the car."

"I'll just put these down and help you bring them in."

"No. No use both of us getting wet." She took a quick scan of the freshly painted teal-colored walls, the deep mauve settee and the leather library chairs. "Coming along."

"You're telling me." Sissy set the paintings down on the coffee table. "I feel like I've been working in a box and someone just opened the lid and let in air. Let me get you an umbrella, at least."

"I wouldn't be able to hold it. Besides, I'm already wet. Be right back."

Savannah dashed out and sprinted the half block to her car. It was a hard, driving rain, but at least it was warm. No one seemed to be worried about a spring drought anymore—as Mrs. Metz had been happy to inform her when they ran into each other at the post office this morning.

The weather, however inconvenient at the moment, was causing Savannah's flowers to thrive.

By the time she got back in with the last of the paintings, she was soaked to the skin and squishing in her shoes.

"Is the boss in?" She set the paintings down, then took off the cap to run her fingers through her damp hair. "He might want to take a look before I hang these."

"He's with a client." Sissy flashed a smile. "But I'm

dying to take a look." She snatched scissors off her desk. "Okay?"

"Sure. You've got to live with them, too."

"I can't believe how fast all this has moved." Quickly she cut the twine on the top bundle. "Once the boss makes up his mind, he moves. No fiddle, no faddle, no— I *love* this!" She ended on a high tone of enthusiasm as she pulled back the heavy paper.

It was a street scene, and the people in it were splashes of vivid color and movement. The buildings were jumbled, giving it a carelessly cheerful theme, and they were awash with lacy balconies, alive with trailing and spreading flowers. On closer inspection, Sissy picked out a toe-tapping fiddler, an enormous black woman in a flowing red caftan, three small boys racing after a yellow dog. She could almost hear the shouts and the music.

"It's wonderful. Tell me this one's going out here."

"That was the idea." Surprised and flattered by the reaction, Savannah dragged a hand through her hair again. "It's New Orleans. The French Quarter. I thought it would liven things up a bit in the waiting area."

"I can't tell you how tired I was of looking at pale pink flowers in a gray vase. I kept hoping I'd come in

one morning and they'd have died during the night."
Sissy chuckled to herself. "Now this I could look at
forever. Did you take art in college?"

The innocent question had Savannah's smile freez-
ing. "No. No, I didn't go to college."

"I had one semester of art," Sissy went on cheerfully,
holding up the painting. "And was told I had absolutely
no sense of perspective. Squeaked by with a C."

When the phone rang, she huffed a bit, then tilted
the painting against the table and went back to her desk
to answer it.

Foolish, foolish, Savannah told herself, to feel inadequate. No, she hadn't gone to college, but she knew
how to paint. Hadn't Sissy's reaction just proven it?

Odd, Savannah thought, that she should still be nervous after her work had been viewed and appreciated.
For most of her life she'd had to convince herself that
painting was—could be—nothing more than a hobby.
A personal indulgence, those times when she'd had to
choose between buying paints and having lunch.

Paints had usually won.

Those days were over. Long over. She'd been in-
credibly lucky with her illustrations, and enjoyed doing
them, intended to continue. But the paintings were her.

Selling bayou scenes and charcoal sketches to tourists was a far cry from selling something that had meant something to her when she saw it, when she painted it.

Smiling and damp-palmed, she dug through the tote she'd brought along for her hammer and measuring tape. She'd already measured the wall on an earlier trip, and now she found the center, marked her spot lightly with a pencil. And waited for Sissy to hang up the phone.

"Should I wait, or can I pound this in there now?" She held up a hanger.

"Now. I'm dying to see it up."

With brisk efficiency, Savannah hammered in the support. The frame was a simple natural cherry—Regan's choice. Savannah had to admit, as she adjusted the painting on the wall, that it had been a good one.

"Bring the left corner up just a tad... Yeah, good." Hands on hips, Sissy nodded. "Good. Perfect. It's about time this place started looking more like the boss and less like..."

"His ex-wife?" Savannah finished, with a glance over her shoulder.

Sissy wrinkled her nose. "Let's just say she was very

low-key. The kind of woman who never has a hair out of place, never raises her voice, never chips a nail."

"She must have had something to have attracted Jared."

Cautious, Sissy cast a look up the steps. "She was beautiful, in that don't-touch-me-I've-just-been-polished sort of way. Very classic, sort of Grace Kelly without the warmth and humor. And she was brilliant. Really. Not only in her profession, but she spoke perfect French, and played the piano beautifully. She read Kafka."

"Oh." Savannah struggled not to frown. She wasn't entirely sure she knew who or what Kafka was, but she was sure she'd never read it.

"In her way, she was admirable. But about as entertaining as a dead frog in a millpond." Sissy beamed at Savannah. "No one can accuse you of that," she said, and, with a quick laugh, picked up the ringing phone.

No, Savannah mused. No one could accuse her of that. Not of being polished or brilliant, or of reading Kafka. She could speak a little French—if you counted the Cajun variety.

Refusing to be intimidated by the image of the

woman Jared had once chosen for his wife, she un-wrapped the next painting.

She hung a trio of small still lifes in the entranceway while Sissy went back to work. While the rain pounded outside and Sissy's keyboard clattered, Savannah began to enjoy the simple pleasure of decorating, of choosing a space and bringing it to life. By the time she'd gotten to the second floor, she was humming under her breath.

Unwilling to hammer there while Jared was with a client, she leaned paintings against the walls she'd cho-sen for them, moving down the hallway and eventually into the office across from Jared's.

The former office, she thought, of the former Mrs. MacKade. No, she remembered. Not Mrs. MacKade. Jared had said she hadn't taken his name.

The walls here were a deep rose, the trim almost a jade, reversing the theme from the lower office. Regan had turned it into a comfortable and efficient sitting room. There was a desk, of course, but there were cozy chairs, tables, books. And, when she poked into a cabi-net, a coffeemaker, cups.

Here, Savannah supposed, Jared could entertain or interview clients in a less formal atmosphere. Or perhaps he could use it to relax, unwind. Or maybe he was considering taking on an associate.

It occurred to her then that she knew very little about his work, or his plans, or what his workday was like.

She'd never asked, Savannah reminded herself—and why should he discuss cases with her? She knew nothing about the law except the problems she'd had with it, fighting to stay one step ahead of the system and keep her child.

He would have discussed them with his wife, she thought, then cursed herself for falling into that typical and pathetic mind-set.

Setting her thoughts on the job at hand again, she stepped out into the hall just as Jared's door opened.

"I'll have a draft of the contract sent out to you in a couple of days," Jared was saying. Then stopped, looked, and smiled. "Hello, Savannah."

"Hello. I'm sorry. I was arranging the paintings."

"You going to introduce me to this beautiful young woman, Jared, or do I have to make my own moves?"

"Savannah Morningstar, Howard Beels."

"Savannah Morningstar. That's a name that suits you." The big, barrel chested man of about fifty shot out a hand the size of a small ham and gripped Savannah's. His eyes, a twinkling blue set in pockets and folds of creased skin, were alight with male admiration. "You working for this shyster?"

"In a manner of speaking." Savannah recognized the look, the squeeze. She'd seen and felt it hundreds of times before, and after a quick survey she judged Howard Beels as harmless. She let her smile warm, because she knew he would take it home with him and sigh. "You hire this shyster, Howard?"

He gave a gut-rattling laugh. "A man needs a clever lawyer in this dirty old world," Howard told her. "Jared here's been mine for, what is it now? Five years?"

"Just about," Jared murmured, intrigued by the easy way Savannah handled, and entertained, one of his top clients.

"What do you do, Howard?"

"Oh, a little of this, a little of that." He had yet to let go of her hand. And he winked. "I'm a dabbler. How about you?"

"I'm a dabbler myself," Savannah told him, and made him laugh again.

"Savannah's an artist," Jared put in. "The next time you come in, Howard, you'll see her work on the walls."

"Is that so?" His sharp eyes homed in on the paint-

ing leaning against the wall behind her. "That your
work there?"

"Yes."

He released her hand to cross to it. Despite his size,
he hunkered down easily to study it. "It's right nice,"
he decided, liking the way the colors flowed and the
way the flowers she'd chosen to paint seemed crowded
together, more alive than perfect. "How much something like this go for?"

Savannah shifted her weight to one hip. "As much
as I think I can get," she said dryly.

Howard slapped his knee appreciatively before he
straightened. "I like this girl, Jared. I'm going to give
you my card, honey." He reached in his jacket pocket
and pulled one out. "You give me a call, hear? I think
we could have ourselves a negotiation over a picture
or two."

"I'll do that Howard." She glanced at the card, but it
gave no clue to his profession. "I'll be sure to do that."

"Don't let any grass grow under your feet, either."
He gave her a last wink before turning to Jared. "I'll
expect those papers."

Savannah smiled at his retreating back. "Quite a
character," she murmured.

"You sure handled him," Jared observed.

"I'm used to handling characters." She tucked the card away. "I've finished downstairs. If I wouldn't be in your way, I could finish up here."

"Sure."

He leaned against the doorway, watching her as she lifted the painting behind her. "A little more to the right," he suggested. "Howard's got an eye for the ladies."

"Yes, I gathered that." Satisfied, Savannah set the painting down and prepared to hammer in the hanger. "And I'd venture to say he's been faithful to his wife for...oh, twenty-five years."

"Twenty-six in May. Three kids, four grandchildren. He has an eye for the ladies," Jared repeated, "but he's one of the shrewdest businessmen I know. Real estate, mostly. Buys and sells. Develops. He owns a couple of small hotels, and the lion's share of a five-star restaurant."

"Really?"

"Hmm... He's on the arts council, works with the Western Maryland Museum."

As the card in her pocket suddenly took on more weight, Savannah nearly bashed her thumb. "That's interesting." Carefully, she set down the hammer. "It looks like I was in the right place at the right time."

"He wouldn't have told you to call him if he didn't mean it. I'm not sure how an artist might feel about having her work in hotels and restaurants and law offices."

She closed her eyes a moment. "I'd feel fine about it." She hung the painting, stepped back to study it. "I'd feel just fine."

"No artistic temperament?"

"I've never been able to afford artistic temperament."

"And if you could?"

"I'd still feel fine about it." She turned then to study his face. "Why wouldn't I?"

"I suppose I'm wondering why you wouldn't want or ask for more."

She wasn't sure it was only art that he was speaking of now. But the answer had to remain the same. "Because I'm happy with what I've got."

His lips curved slowly as he reached out to touch her face. "You're a complicated woman, Savannah, and amazingly simple. It's a fascinating mix. Why don't I take you to lunch?"

"That's a nice offer, but I want to get this done. If

you're going, I could hang the pieces in your office while you're out."

"Why don't I stay, and we can order in? I'll watch you hang the pieces in my office."

"That would work." She tucked her restless hands into her pockets, then pulled them out. "Actually, there's something I'd like you to see. You didn't pick it, but I thought if you liked it, you might want it in your office."

Curious, he watched the nerves jitter in her eyes. "Let's take a look."

"Okay." She walked down the hallway to where she'd left the painting, still wrapped. "If you don't like it, it's no big deal." She shrugged and shifted past him to carry it into his office herself. "Either way, it's a gift." She set it on his desk, stepped away, jammed her hands into her pockets again. "No charge."

"A present?" He stroked a hand over her shoulder as he went to the desk for scissors to cut the twine.

The idea of a present from her delighted him. But when he folded back the protective paper and saw it, the quick smile faded. And Savannah's heart sank.

The woods were deep and thick, filled with mystery and moonlight. Black trunks, gnarled, burled, rose up into twisted branches that held leaves just unfurled with spring. There were hints of color. Wild azalea and dogwood gleamed in that ghostly light. The rocky ground was carpeted with leaves that had fallen the autumn before, and the autumn before that, a sign of the continuous ebb and flow of life.

He could see the trio of rocks where he often sat, the fallen trunk where he had once sat with her. And in the distance, just a hint through the shadows, was a glow of light that signaled his home.

For a moment, he wasn't sure he could speak. "When did you do this?"

"I just finished it a few days ago." A mistake, she thought, cursing herself. A sentimental, foolish mistake. "It's just something I've worked on in my spare time. Like I said, it's no big deal. If you don't like it—"

Before she could finish, his head came up, and his eyes, swirling with emotion, met hers. "I can't think of anything I've ever been given that could mean more. It's the way it looked the night we made love for the first time. The way it's looked countless times I've been there alone."

Her heart stuttered, then crept up to lodge in her throat. "I was going to paint it the way it would have been in autumn, during the battle. But I wanted to do it this way first. I wasn't sure you'd… I'm glad you like it."

He reached out, cupped her face in his hands. "I love you, Savannah."

Her lips curved under the gentle caress of his, then parted, heated, as he steadily deepened the kiss. His fingers tangled in her hair, still damp from the rain. Her arousal was slow and sweet.

"I should hang it for you."

"Mmm…" Quite suddenly, as her body pressed to his and her mouth began to move, he had a much better idea. He tucked an arm around her to hold her steady and reached over his desk to pick up the phone. "Sissy? Why don't you go to lunch now? Yeah, take your time."

Savannah's gaze followed his hand as he replaced the receiver. Then her eyes shifted blandly to his face. "If you think you're going to seduce me here in your office, have me rolling over your fancy new carpet with you while your secretary's out to lunch…"

Jared walked over, closed the door. Locked it. Arched a brow. "Yes?"

She tossed her hair back, leaned a hip on the desk. "You're absolutely right."

He shrugged off his jacket, hung it on the brass coat

hook by the door. His tie followed. Keeping his eyes on hers, he crossed back. One by one, he loosened the buttons of her shirt.

"Your clothes are damp."

"It's raining."

Very slowly, very deliberately, he peeled the bright cotton away. His eyes never left hers as he slipped a finger under the front hook of her bra. Never left hers when he felt the quick quiver of her skin and heard the little catch in her breathing.

"I want you every time I see you. I want you when I don't see you." With a flick of his thumb and forefinger, he unsnapped the hook. "I want you even after I've had you." Lightly he traced his fingertips over the curve of her breast. "You obsess me, Savannah, the way no one and nothing ever has."

She reached out for him, but he shook his head and lowered her arms to her sides again. "No, let me. Just let me."

His thumbs brushed over her nipples, his eyes stayed focused on her face. "I lose my mind when I touch you," he murmured. "This time I want to watch you lose yours."

Fingers, thumbs, palms, cruised over her. Rough,

then gentle, tender, then demanding, as if he was refusing to let any one mood rule. Driven, she pulled at him, tried to tug him closer. But each time she did, he stopped, patiently lowered her arms until she had no choice but to grip the edge of the desk and let him have his way.

No one had ever made love to her like this, as if she were essential, as if she were all there was and all there needed to be. As if her pleasure were paramount. Pinpoint sensations percolated along her skin, chased by others, whisper-soft, then still more that seeped slyly through flesh to blood and bone.

She arched back on a keening moan when he closed his teeth over her, shot her to some rugged ground on the border between pleasure and pain.

"Just take me." Her arms whipped around him, her body straining, pulsing.

But he took her hands, locked them to his as he kissed her toward delirium. Her mouth was a feast, full of hot flavor and a hunger that matched his own. But this time he wasn't content to sink into it, or her. He used his teeth to torment, his tongue to tease, until her breath came in tearing gasps.

"Let me touch you," she demanded.

"Not this time. Not yet." He closed her hands over the edge of the desk again, held them there while his mouth raced to her throat, down her neck, over those tensed and beautiful shoulders. "I'm going to take you, Savannah." He eased back, because he wanted her to see his face, and the unshakable purpose there. "I'm going to take you inch by inch. The way no one ever has."

For her pleasure, he told himself. But he knew a part of it was his own pride. He wanted to show her that no man before, and no man after, could make her feel what he could.

So he showed her, traveling like lightning down her torso, her flesh damp now, not from rain, but from passion.

She gave herself over to him as she had never done with any man. Surrender complete, she braced herself on the desk and let him ravage her, body and mind.

He tugged off her shoes. She let her head fall back, let herself moan deep as he eased her jeans low on her hips, caressed that revealed flesh with his lips. She shuddered, nearly sobbed, as his hands kneaded and his mouth closed over her, fire to fire.

She crested fast and hard. Terrifying. Wonderful. He never stopped, and as the pleasure whipped her ruthlessly higher, she prayed he never would. Naked, stripped of clothes and all defenses, she could do nothing but experience, absorb and give.

He'd never known this kind of desire. To take and to take, knowing as he did that he was filling her with unspeakable pleasure. The blood swam in his head as he felt her peak yet again, heard that breathless cry catch in her throat.

The strong muscles in her legs were quivering. He ran his tongue over them, lingering over the symbol she'd branded herself with, before making his way, purposely, greedily, up that long body.

Her eyes were closed. He used his mouth only to keep her poised and ready for him as he stripped off his shirt. He toed off his shoes, whipped his trousers aside. And dragged her to the floor.

The animal that had been pacing restlessly inside him sprang free. He drove himself into her, mindlessly, shuddering with a dark thrill when she cried out his name, hissing with hot pleasure as her nails scraped his back.

It was all heat and speed and plunging bodies, a rhythmic, tribal beat of flesh against flesh. The blood hammered in his head, his heart, his loins, relentlessly. She arched up to him, straining, straining.

His vision grayed, his world contracted. He emptied himself into her.

Savannah thought, if she really tried, she might be able to crawl to where her clothes were heaped. And she would try, she told herself. In just another minute or two.

Right now, it was so lovely and decadent to lie there on the antique carpet in Jared's quietly elegant office with his body heavy on hers.

She had been, she realized, thoroughly and mind-numbingly ravished. As exciting as making love with him had been before, this was a different level entirely. She certainly hoped they would strive for it now and again in the future.

"I have to get up," she murmured.

"Why?"

"To make certain I'm not paralyzed."

"Did I hurt you?"

She kept her eyes closed, let her lips curve. "Another few minutes of that, and you'd have killed me." Making the effort, she found the energy to stroke a hand through his hair. "Thank you."

"Anytime." He let out a long, heartfelt sigh before he pressed a kiss to her throat. "Of course, I don't know how I'm ever going to work in here again." Moaning a little, he rolled off her. "I'll have a client sitting in the chair while I go over the details of his case, and I'll get a flash of you leaning naked against the desk."

She laughed, then discovered she really did have to crawl. Her legs might never support her again. "He'll get suspicious when you get a stupid grin on your face."

"And start drooling." Spent, Jared reached for his shirt. He angled his head to get a glimpse of her tattoo. "Hell of a way to kick off the new color scheme."

"Didn't you ever kick off the old one?"

He had to concentrate on remembering how to button his shirt, so it took him a minute. The snort of laughter came first. "You mean me and Barbara? I'm not sure she ever unbuttoned her double-breasted blazer in here. Not her style."

In her underwear, Savannah turned to study him. "You *were* married to her, right?"

"That's what it said on the license."

"Why?"

"It has to say that. It's the law."

"Why were you married to her?"

"We had a lot in common. I thought." He shrugged it off. "We both wanted to establish ourselves in our respective professions, knew a lot of the same people, attended a lot of the same functions."

It disturbed him still how empty it sounded when he pulled things apart and looked at all the pieces. "She was a sensible, reasonable and sophisticated woman. That's what I wanted—or thought I did. A kind of contrast to the hotheaded-troublemaker image I'd carved out for myself when I was younger."

"You wanted dignity." Still sitting on the floor, Savannah buttoned her shirt.

"That's accurate enough. It seemed important then."

"It's still important. It always is." Though she realized it would sound a bit foolish while she tugged herself into her jeans, she said it anyway. "I always wanted it, too. Not in the double-breasted-suit sort of way. Not *my* style. Just in the way people look at you, what they see when they do."

She pulled on a shoe. "That's why I like living here. I can start fresh."

"We all look back." He walked over to the coatrack for his tie. "It's human nature."

"I don't." She said it almost fiercely as she pulled on the second shoe. "Not anymore."

He gave his full attention to the tying of his tie. "There's no one? Of all the people you've known, the people who've touched you?"

She started to answer lightly, but then it struck her. He didn't mean people. He meant men. And she remembered what he had said as he made love to her, made her churn and shiver.

The way no one ever has.

And so, she thought, hurt, that was the crux of it. "You mean lovers."

"You said lovers. I said people."

"I know what you said, Jared. No, there's no one who was important enough to look back to."

Bryan's father. He nearly said it, nearly asked, but it stuck in his throat. In his pride. "You're angry," he stated, noting the glint in her eye.

"It just crossed my mind that what happened here was a kind of demonstration. A chest-beating male sort of thing, to illustrate that you're better than anyone I might have had before."

Now his own eyes glinted. "That's a remarkably stupid observation."

"Don't tell me I'm stupid." She snapped it out, then managed to pull herself back under control. Don't let it matter, she reminded herself. Don't let it sting. "You can relax, Jared, you proved your point. You're an extraordinary lover. Right over the top." She sauntered over to brush a hand over his tensed jaw. "I enjoyed every minute of it. But now I don't have time to hang your paintings. I've got some errands to run before I head back home."

He put a hand on her arm. He understood her well enough now to know that careless arrogance was one of her ways of covering anger. "I think we have something to talk about."

"It'll have to wait." Reaching behind him, she flipped open the lock. "We've eaten up your lunch hour, and I imagine Sissy'll be breezing back any minute." She gave him a light, careless kiss before shaking her arm free.

"We have something to talk about," he repeated.

"Fine. You get it all worked out in your head, and we'll talk about it tonight." Knowing she was goading him, she curved her lips in a cocky smile. "Thanks for the demonstration, MacKade. It was memorable."

She wouldn't have gotten two feet if Sissy hadn't rushed in below. "Hey, Savannah," she called up cheerfully. "The way it's coming down out there, you're going to want to trade your car in for an ark."

"Then I'd better get moving," Savannah said, and walked down the stairs without looking back.

Chapter 11

He bought flowers. Jared wasn't sure whether he was apologizing or he'd simply gotten into the habit of picking them up once or twice a week because Savannah always looked so surprised and pleased when he walked in with a bouquet.

He didn't like to think the clutch of late-spring blooms was an apology, because he didn't think he'd been completely wrong. Technically, he hadn't asked; he'd only intimated a question. And why the hell shouldn't he ask?

He wanted to know more about her, the who and

what and why of her past. Not just the pieces she let drop from time to time, but the whole picture.

Of course, his timing and delivery had been poor. He could admit that. He could even admit that it had nipped at his temper that she'd seen through him so easily. But the bottom line was, he had a right to know. They were going to have a calm, reasonable talk about just that.

Perhaps because he was so primed, so ready, he found himself simmering when he drove up the lane and saw that her car was gone.

Where the hell was she? It was after six. He stood by his car, frowning, looking over the land. The rain had left the tumbling flowers on the bank vivid and wet. The azaleas she'd planted had lost most of their blossoms, but their leaves were a rich and glossy green.

He remembered the first day he'd seen her, digging in the earth, with pots of flowers surrounding her and the rocky, neglected bank waiting.

She'd done something here, he thought. Those roots she'd talked about were still shallow, but she'd dug them in. He needed to believe that she had made that commitment, and found comfort in the green of the grass she preferred to mow herself, in the mixed colors of the blooms she tended religiously, in the woods beyond that they both seemed to share on such a deep, personal level.

He saw Bryan's bike standing beside the walkway, a bright orange Frisbee that had ended its flight in the middle of the sloping lawn, a wheelbarrow full of mulch parked beside the porch.

Details, he mused, little details that made a home.

And it hit him suddenly and forcefully that he wanted, needed, it to be his home. Not just a place where he left a few of his things so that it was convenient to spend the night. Home.

He didn't want Savannah to be just the woman he loved and made love with. He'd failed at marriage once, and had been sure, so sure, that he would never put himself in the position where he could fail at something so personal and public again. Hadn't he told himself he would be content to drift along in this relationship?

But he'd been lying to himself almost from the beginning, because he hadn't been content and didn't want to drift. So he poked at her, prodded, subtly and not so subtly, for those answers to who she was, where she'd been. While part of him, the part that was pride and heart, was wounded every time she didn't simply volunteer the answers.

He wanted her to confide in him, to share with him every part of her that had been, that was, that would be. He needed her to turn to him when she was troubled or sad, or when she was happy.

He wanted, Jared realized, drawing a slow, steady breath. He wanted her to marry him, have children with him, grow old with him.

He started up the walkway, pausing to lay a hand on Bryan's bike. He wanted the boy. That, too, was fresh and revealing news. He didn't want Bryan to be Savannah's son, but their son. Helping Bryan with his homework, boning up on baseball, cheering from the bleachers at a game. Jared realized he'd gotten used to those things, looked forward to them. Looked forward to that quick grin, the shouted greeting.

But it wasn't enough. It didn't make them family.

Love would. He'd grown to love the boy in a very short time, without even realizing it. Marriage would. Not just the legal contract, Jared reflected. The promise.

⋅ He and Barbara had broken that promise, and had proceeded to negate the legal contract without flinching with another. All very clean, very tidy, very civilized.

Wasn't that the core of it? There was nothing very civilized about the way he felt about Savannah or

Bryan. He felt protective, proprietary, possessive. They were difficult emotions. Untidy emotions.

Wonderful.

Calmer now that he'd sorted through the problem, and its solution, he went into the house.

There were shoes where there shouldn't be, books and glasses and toys scattered instead of in their proper place. A pair of earrings tossed on a table, a trail of mud that hadn't been quite scraped off on the mat.

It was home.

But where the hell were they?

He'd grown accustomed to finding them there. Bryan in the yard, or poring over his baseball-card collection in his room. The radio should have been blaring, or the TV turned up too loud. She should have been in the kitchen, or in her little studio in the back, or taking one of her cat naps on the sofa.

He went into the kitchen, laid the flowers down on the table. No note. No hastily scrawled explanation tacked to the refrigerator. Frowning, he laid his brief-case beside the flowers. The least she could have done was leave him a note.

They'd agreed to talk, hadn't they? He had reams to talk about, and she wasn't even here. He looked in her studio. A half glass of watered-down lemonade stood on her worktable near a clever, sly sketch of a flying frog.

Under other circumstances, it would have made him smile.

His mood darkening by the minute, he headed upstairs. Dragging off his tie, he walked into her bedroom. *Her* bedroom, he thought, sizzling. By God, that was going to change. He tossed the tie on the bed, followed it with his suit jacket.

They were going to have a long, serious discussion, he and Savannah. And she was going to listen.

He grumbled to himself as he changed into jeans and hung his suit in the closet amid her clothes. His teeth were set. One of the first things they were going to do was add another closet. A man deserved his own damn closet.

In fact, they were going to add on another bedroom, one big enough for his things, as well as hers. And another bathroom, while they were at it, because they were going to have more children.

And an office. She wasn't the only one who needed work space.

Then he was going to build Bryan a tree house. The kid should have a tree house.

They needed a garden shed for her tools, and the lane needed work. Well, he would see to those things. He'd see to them because... He was going insane, Jared admitted, and sat down on the edge of the bed.

He hadn't even told her they were getting married, and he already he was adding on to the house.

What was he getting so worked up about? Why was he so angry with her, with himself? Panic, he wondered. Little licks of fear. Worry that when he mentioned marriage, she would laugh and tell him that wasn't the kind of thing that interested her.

Dragging his hands through his hair, he rose. She was going to have to get interested, he decided. And fast.

He might have calmed again, might have gone reasonably downstairs and started dinner for the three of them. He might have done that. It was in his mind when he noticed the box on her dresser.

He caught the glint of belt buckles. Big, showy buckles. Rodeo. He lifted one and studied the embossed horse and rider. Her father's things. She'd received her father's assets. And she hadn't told him.

There wasn't much. The prizes Jim Morningstar had won years before, bits and pieces of a man who had obviously traveled light and without too much sentiment. There was a larger box beside the dresser. Old, worn boots, a battered hat, a few articles of clothing that were still folded, as if she hadn't touched them.

He saw the letter from his colleague in Oklahoma, the standard cover for the dispensation of effects, the itemized list, the offer to assist if there were any questions.

Jared shifted it aside. And found the photographs.

Most were crinkled, as if they'd been carelessly shoved in drawers, badly packed in a move. He saw Jim Morningstar for the first time. An impressive candid shot of a man, face hard and set, eyes narrowed as he sat a horse in a high, narrow stall.

The dark coloring, the high cheekbones Savannah had inherited. But there was little else in this tough, leathery face that had been passed to her, unless it was the set of that chin, he mused. The set that warned that if life aimed a fist, this one would meet it straight on.

He found another, poorly framed, of the same man standing beside a young Savannah. Jared's lips curved as he studied her. She was maybe thirteen, fourteen, he thought. Tall, her body, tucked into jeans and a plaid shirt, already curving, her hair raining out of a cowboy hat.

She looked straight at the camera, her lips hinting at that knowing woman's smile she'd have in later life. She stood hip-shot, a certain arrogance in the stance. One of her hands rested lightly on her father's shoulder. Jim Morningstar had his arms folded over his chest. He didn't touch his daughter.

There was another of Savannah, a still younger Savannah, astride a horse. It was a classic pose, the buckskin-colored horse rearing up, the rider with her hat swept off her head and lifted high in one hand.

She looked, Jared thought, as if she would dare anything.

There were more of Morningstar with other men— grinning, leather-faced men in hats and boots and denim. Backgrounds of corrals, stables, horses. Always horses.

It played through his mind that they might clear space for a paddock, use the barn at the farm and get a horse or two. Savannah obviously loved them, and Bryan might—

Every thought leaked out of his head as he stared at the last photo.

Yes, she would have been about sixteen, though her body was fully a woman's, clad in a snug T-shirt tucked into tight jeans. Yet the face had a softness, a slight fullness that announced that the girl hadn't quite finished becoming a woman yet. She was laughing. The camera had frozen her in that full-throated moment. He could almost hear it.

She was wrapped around a man. And the man was wrapped around her. Their arms were entwined, their faces were laughing at the camera. The man's hat was pushed back on his head, revealing curls of shaggy blond hair. He was tanned, lean, tall. His eyes would have been blue, or perhaps green. It was hard to tell from the snapshot. But they were light, the corners crinkled with the smile.

The mouth that was cocked crookedly in that smile had been passed on to Bryan.

This was Bryan's father.

Jared felt his anger begin to pulse. This was the man. A man, he repeated in his head, not a boy. The face was undeniably handsome, even striking, but it didn't belong to a teenager. This man had seduced a sixteen-year-old girl, then abandoned her. And nothing had been done.

Morningstar had kept the photo. Because, Jared thought with a tight-lipped snarl, he'd known.

And nothing had been done.

Savannah watched him from the doorway. Her emotions had been on a roller coaster all day. This looked like one more dip.

She'd wanted to forget the edginess, the anger she'd felt when she left Jared's office. She'd hoped to come home, find him here and share with him her small triumph in selling Howard Beels three paintings.

With a very good possibility of more.

She and Bryan had cackled about it all the way home. Over Howard himself and the way he'd hemmed and hawed over what she considered a highly inflated asking price, and settled on an amount that had been considerably more than she'd anticipated.

She'd even stopped off and bought a bottle of champagne so that she and Jared could celebrate. So that she could celebrate with him the fact that her long-buried wish of painting for a living was working its way to the surface.

But she could see there would be no celebration now.

Not with that look on Jared's face as he studied what her father had left her. She didn't know where his anger came from. But she had a feeling she was going to find out.

The hell with it, she thought, and pushed away from the door jamb. Let's get it over with.

"Not much of an estate, huh?" She waited until his head came up, until his gaze shifted to hers. The fury in them almost buckled her knees. "I imagine most of your clients have a bit more to deal with."

He knew how to take things one step at a time, to start at one point and work his way to the heart. "When did you get the shipment?"

"A week or two ago." She shrugged, then walked over to the window to look down. "Bry's down in the yard. We picked up the kittens. He's in heaven."

Jared MacKade also knew how to stay on a point. "A week or two. You didn't mention it."

"What was to mention? I took out the check and gave it to that broker you recommended. I didn't feel like dealing with the rest, so I put it aside until this morning. I guess I'll put the buckles away for Bryan. He might want them one day. The clothes'll go to charity, I suppose."

"Why didn't you tell me?"

"Why should I have?" She turned back, vaguely annoyed, vaguely curious. "It's not a big deal. No long-lost lottery tickets or pouch of gold dust. Just some old clothes, older boots, and papers."

"And photographs."

"Yeah, a few. He wasn't big on souvenirs. There's one of him in the chute I like. It shows who he was, always gearing up for the next ride. I figured Bryan might like to have that, too."

"And this one?" Jared held up the snapshot of Savannah and the cockily smiling cowboy.

She lifted a brow, shook her head. "I don't know how I got into those jeans. Look, I'm going to throw some burgers on the grill."

When Jared shifted into her path, she was genuinely surprised. She tilted her head, studied him. And waited. "Have you shown this to Bryan?"

"No."

"Do you intend to?"

"No. I don't think he cares what his mother looked like at sixteen."

"He would care what his father looked like."

She could almost feel her blood slow, go sluggish. "He doesn't have a father."

"Damn it, Savannah, are you going to tell me this isn't Bryan's father?"

"I'm going to tell you that isn't Bryan's father. A couple of rolls in the hay doesn't make a man a father."

"Don't slice words with me."

"It's a very important distinction in my book, Lawyer MacKade. And since this seems to be a cross-examination, I'll make it clear and easy. I had sex with the man in the picture you're holding. I got pregnant. End of story."

"The hell it is." Furious, he slapped the picture down on the dresser. "Your father knew. He wouldn't have kept this, otherwise."

"Yeah. That occurred to me when I found it." And the hurt had come with it, but it had been slight and easily dispatched. "So what?"

"So why wasn't anything done? This isn't a kid we're talking about. He had to be over twenty-one."

"I think he was twenty-four. Maybe twenty-five. It's hard to remember."

"And you were a minor. He should have been prosecuted—after your father broke his neck."

Savannah took a deep breath. "In the first place, my father knew me. He knew that if I'd slept with someone, it was my choice. I was a minor, technically, but I knew exactly what I was doing. It wasn't a mistake or an accident. I wasn't forced. And I don't appreciate you casting blame."

"Of course there's blame," Jared shot back. "That son of a bitch had no right touching a girl your age, then taking off when there were consequences."

Her eyes lit. "Bryan is not a consequence."

"You know damn well that's not what I meant." Pulling both hands through his hair, he paced away. "There's no going back and righting wrongs at this point. I want to know what you intend to do now."

"I intend to cook hamburgers. You're welcome to stay, or you're welcome to go."

"Don't take that attitude with me."

"It's the attitude I've got." Then she sighed. "Jared, why are you gnawing at this thing? I slept with a man ten years ago. I forgot him. He forgot me." To illustrate, she picked up the photo and dropped it carelessly in the wastebasket beside the dresser. "That's that."

"Just that simple?" It was that, Jared realized.

Exactly that that gnawed at him. "He didn't mean anything to you?"

"That's right."

"You conceived a child with him, Savannah. That boy who's down in the yard, playing with his kittens. How can you just dismiss that?"

Temper streaked through her. "You'd prefer a different story, wouldn't you, Jared? A different story you could live with. One about the poor, innocent, neglected girl looking for love, seduced by an older man, betrayed, abandoned."

"Isn't that what happened?"

"You don't know who I was, what I was, or what I wanted. You don't want to know, not really. Because when you do, when you hear it, it'll stick in your craw. How many men has she been with? Can I believe her when she tells me she didn't sell herself? Even her own father didn't stand by her, so what does that tell me? Now that I look back, I remember she was ready to hit the sheets with me from the get-go. What kind of a woman have I got myself tangled up with? Isn't that what you're wondering, Jared?"

"I'm wondering why there are so many things you don't tell me. Why you shrug off ten years of your life and how they affected you. And, yes, I'm wondering what kind of woman you are."

She threw her head back. "Figure it out." She started to storm out, then came up hard, toe-to-toe with him. "Keep out of my way."

"I'm in your way, and you're in mine. And it's long past time to settle this. You say you love me, but you pull back every time I touch a nerve, every time I want a clear picture of what brought you to this point in your life."

"I brought me here. That's all you need to know."

"It's not all I need to know. You can't build a future without drawing on the past."

"I can. I have. If you can't, Jared, it's your problem. You know what you're doing?" She tossed the question at him. "You're harping on a face in a photograph. You're insulted by it, threatened by it."

"That's ridiculous."

"Is it? It's all right for you to have been married before, to have had other women in your life. I haven't asked you how many or who or why, have I? It's all right for you to have been wild and reckless, to have sauntered around town with your brothers, looking for trouble or making it. That's just dandy. Boys will be boys. But with me, it's different. The problem is, you got tangled up with me before you thought it through. Now you want to shift the pieces around, see if you can make me into more of what seems suitable to the man you are now."

"You're putting words in my mouth. And you're wrong."

"I say I'm right. And I say the hell with you, MacKade. The hell with you. You want a victim, or you want a flower, or someone who looks just right at some fundraiser or professional event. You've come to the wrong place. I don't read Kafka."

"What in the sweet hell are you talking about?"

"I'm talking about reality. The reality is, I don't need this kind of grief from you."

His eyes narrowed. "It's not just about what you need. Not anymore. That's reality, Savannah. I don't have to justify wanting to know how you could toss out that photograph, or dismiss your father's things and not even tell me you had them. I don't have to justify asking you what you want from yourself, from me. From us. Or telling you what I want, what I expect and intend to have. That's everything. Everything or nothing."

"Down to ultimatums, are we?"

"Looks that way. Think about it," he suggested, and strode furiously out.

Steaming, she stood where she was. She listened to the door slam below. It took every ounce of willpower she had not to race to the window, to watch him. Maybe to call him back. Minutes later, she heard the sound of his car.

So, that was that, Savannah thought. All or nothing. He had a nerve, demanding she give him all, leave herself nothing to fall back on. Nothing to cushion a fall. She'd been there once, and the bruises had plagued her for years. By God, she wasn't going back.

Steadying herself, she went downstairs. She ignored the flowers on the table, the champagne chilling in the refrigerator. Maybe she'd drink it herself later, she mused as she took out some hamburger. Maybe she'd drink the whole damn bottle and get herself a nice fizzy buzz. It would be better than thinking, better than hurting. Better even than this simmering anger that was still hot in her blood.

But when the door slammed and she looked around she hated herself for the stab of disappointment when she realized it was her son.

"Is Jared mad at you?"

"Why?"

"I could tell." Uneasy, Bryan sat down, propped his elbows on the table. "He stopped to look at the kittens and stuff, but he wasn't paying attention. And he said he couldn't stay."

"I guess he's mad at me."

"Are you mad at him, too?"

"Yeah." Slapping patties together was a fine way to release a little violence. "Pretty mad."

"Does that mean you're not stuck on him anymore?"

She looked over, and her own temper cleared enough that she could see the worry in Bryan's eyes. "What are you getting at, Bry?"

He moved his shoulders, kicked his feet. "Well, you've never been stuck on anybody before. He's mostly always here, and he brings you flowers and hangs around with me. You kiss each other and stuff."

"That's true."

"Well, Con and I thought maybe you were going to get, like, married."

A quick arrow shot straight into her heart. "Oh."

"I thought it would be kind of cool, you know, because Jared's cool."

She put the patties aside. To give herself time, she ran

water, washed her hands and dried them thoroughly. All the while, all she could think was, what had she done to her little boy?

"Bry, you know that people kiss each other all the time without getting married. You're smart enough to know that adults have relationships, close relationships, without getting married, either."

"Yeah, but if they're really stuck on each other, they do, right?"

"Sometimes." She skirted the table to lay a hand on his shoulder. "But it's not always enough to love someone."

"How come?"

"Because…" Where was the answer? "Because people are complicated. Anyway, Jared's mad at me, not at you. You can still be pals."

"I guess."

"You'd better go out and make sure those kittens keep out of trouble. I'm going to fire up the grill."

"Okay." He dragged his feet a little as he started toward the door. "I was thinking if you got married, he'd be sort of like…"

"Sort of like what?" she asked.

"Sort of like my father." Bryan moved his shoulders

again, in a gesture so very much like her own when she blocked off hurt, another shaft of pain shot through her. "I just thought it would be cool."

Chapter 12

Bryan's wistful statement dragged at her mind and spirits all through the evening. To make it up to him for a disappointment she felt unable to control, she made the casual meal into their own private celebration.

All the soda he could drink, french fries made from scratch, wild, involved and ridiculous plans on how they would spend the fortune they would amass from selling her paintings.

Trips to Disney World weren't enough, they decided. They would *own* Disney World. Box seats at ball games? For pikers. They would purchase the Baltimore Orioles—and Bryan would, naturally, play at short.

Savannah kept up the game until she was reasonably sure both of them had forgotten that what Bryan really wanted was Jared.

Then she spent the night staring at the ceiling, thinking of all the wonderful, hideous ways to pay Jared MacKade back for putting a dent in her boy's heart.

Hers wasn't all that important. She knew how to hammer it out. Time and work and the home she'd continue to make would all help. She didn't need a man to make her whole. Never had. She would see to it that her son never felt the lack of a father. But she would punish Jared for raising Bryan's hopes.

The bastard had made himself part of their lives. Flowers, damn him. Playing catch in the yard, taking Bryan over to the farm, awakening her in bed the way no one, damn him again, no one ever had.

Then looking down at her from his lofty lawyer's height. Questioning her morals and her actions and her motives. Making her feel more, then making her feel less, than she'd ever been. Making her question herself.

He wasn't going to get away with it. Without realizing it, she shifted to the center of the bed, so that it wouldn't feel so empty. He couldn't worm his way into their lives, then start making demands. Who was she, where had she been, what did she want? She didn't owe him any answers, and she was going to prove it.

He'd wormed his way in, all right, she thought, scowling at the ceiling. He'd made her feel foolish and inadequate and, for the first time in ten very long years, vulnerable. Now he thought he could worm his way out again because she wasn't just exactly what he preferred in a…

She sneered at the word. In a *wife*.

She hated him for that, really hated him for making her start to think, start to hope and even plan along those lines, without her even being aware of it. Until Bryan brought it up, she hadn't realized she was dreaming, just a little, about happy-ever-after.

Like the fairy tales she illustrated, with their strong and passionate princes.

It was embarrassing. It was humiliating. A woman like her, a woman who had managed through sheer will and grit to shrug off the bruises life handed out, to be brought this low by a man.

She'd survived alone. She'd gone hungry, worked until she was dizzy with fatigue, had taken jobs that scraped at her pride. She'd been turned out by her own father when she needed him most.

And none of that, not one of the painful or difficult experiences in her life, had ever left her as low as this.

And none of that, she had made certain, had ever brought Bryan one moment's sadness.

She took a deep breath, then another. She would show Jared MacKade just what kind of woman she was. The kind of woman who didn't need him.

Jared decided brooding on the front porch with a beer on a Saturday afternoon wasn't such a bad thing. He was almost enjoying it. It was a beautiful day, and he was pleasantly fatigued from the morning's work.

His brothers were with him, and it was a good feeling, to have all of them there. Just passing an hour, he mused, at home. Watching the grass grow and the dogs race over it.

Maybe, just maybe, in a little while, he'd stroll on over to the cabin. He figured he'd given her time enough to stew, to calm down and see reason.

He'd given himself almost enough time, as well. He was almost ready, not quite but almost ready, to admit he'd been somewhat heavy-handed. Maybe just the slightest bit unreasonable.

Still, she'd been ridiculous. Accusing him of being

threatened by a photograph, of wanting a different kind of woman. Of not being satisfied with her because she didn't read Kafka.

God knew where she'd come up with that.

He didn't appreciate the comparison of her life with his, either. Made him sound like a narrow-minded sexist. Which he certainly was not.

It was different, that was all.

"Talking to himself," Devin commented as he whittled a piece of wood.

"Been doing it since he got here yesterday." Shane yawned and kicked back in his chair. "You ask me, Savannah kicked his butt out."

That, and Rafe's snorting laugh, snagged Jared's attention. "She did not. I left to make a point."

"Yeah." Rafe winked at Devin. "What point was that?"

Eyes narrowed, Jared tipped back his beer. "That she'd better start seeing things the way they are."

This statement was greeted by hoots.

"His way," Rafe pointed out. "It always has to be his way or no way."

"Bull." Unoffended, Jared crossed his ankles. "It just has to be the right way."

From his perch on the top step, Devin shifted, leaned his back against the post. "So, what was she doing wrong?"

"She holds back. I get a call from Howard Beels this morning, thanking me for introducing them. Seems she went over there yesterday and he bought three of her paintings." Just thinking of it had him simmering again. "Does she tell me? No. What kind of relationship is that? I don't get anything out of her without a direct question, and then she only answers half the time."

Amused, Shane stretched his arms. "And I just bet you've been full of questions, too. What happened then? What did you do? What chain of events led to that? And where were you on the night in question?"

Jared's punch would have been stronger if Shane hadn't been a full arm's length away. "I don't interrogate her. I ask. I want to know about her. A man has a right to know the woman he's going to marry."

Rafe choked on a gulp of beer. "When did that happen?"

"I knew it." With a heavy sigh, Shane flipped the top of the cooler and got out a beer for himself. "I just knew it."

Eyes bland, Devin studied Jared. "You asked Savannah to marry you?"

"No. I didn't get a chance to tell her—"

"Tell her." Now Devin grinned. "Typical."

"You might try to see my side of it," Jared grumbled. "I realized that's what I want. I was thinking about it, going over it, and then I see she's gotten the effects from her father. She hadn't told me it had come. There was a photograph of her with Bryan's father."

"Hmm…" Rafe's comment went for all of them.

"When I asked her about it, she got defensive."

"Hostile witness," Shane murmured, and earned a glare.

"She tossed it out," Jared continued. "Like it meant nothing."

"Maybe that's just what it meant," Devin put in.

"Look, the bastard got her pregnant, then abandoned her. Her father kicks her out. She's sixteen, for God's sake. It means something. But she won't come out with it. She won't tell me. What she does is start accusing me of idiotic things. Then she says, get this, she says that I figure it was all right for me to sow wild oats or whatever, to get in trouble and kick some butt. But I expect her to be untouched or a victim, or words to that effect. It's insulting."

Rafe regarded the lip of his beer bottle. "It's true."

"The hell it is."

"Sorry, bro. You pass the bar, buy yourself a couple of lawyer suits—"

"Do you want me to break your nose again?"

"In a minute. Anyway, after a while you decide it's time to get married, so you pick out an ice queen, one with no baggage, no secrets, no noticeable flaws. You know why?"

Temper percolating, Jared eyed him. "Why don't you tell me?"

"Because the image worked for you. It didn't take you long to realize the woman didn't, because you're pretty sharp most of the time. Now, Savannah, there's a woman with baggage, some secrets, a few flaws. The image is a little hard to tuck into a box, but the woman works."

He wanted to argue, to debate, to tear the hypothesis to shreds. And discovered he couldn't. So he swore instead.

"Kafka," he muttered as a light dawned. "Barbara read Kafka."

"Doesn't surprise me," Rafe said cheerfully.

Trying it all from a new angle, Jared took out a cigar. "The argument is still valid that if two people want to build a future together, they have to trust each other enough to share the past. I want the boy, too," he said, blowing out a stream of smoke.

"Are you going to let a photograph stop you?" Devin asked quietly.

"No. I'm not going to let anything stop me."

"Two down," Shane complained. "You know, women start getting ideas when your brothers get married."

"Live with it," Jared told him.

All of them glanced over at the sound of a car coming up the lane, fast.

So she'd come to her senses, he decided, proud of the fact that he'd given her the night to think it over. Now she was here, sorry she'd lost her temper, he imagined. Ready to sit down and discuss it all reasonably.

He rose, moved over to lean on the post opposite Devin. He'd be big enough to apologize, as well, he thought. And to explain himself more coherently. He was sure that years from now they'd laugh over the whole foolish mess.

He lifted the cigar to his lips, ready to welcome her, when she squealed to a halt at the end of the lane.

The woman who unfolded herself from the car didn't look conciliatory. She looked wild, glowing and stunning.

"Oh-oh" was all Shane said, but he rolled his eyes merrily at Rafe.

She didn't speak, but stood with her hands on her hips, scanning the four men. An audience, she thought. Even better. Didn't they all look smug and pleased with themselves just for being men?

She swaggered around to the trunk, unlocked it. The box came first. The dogs jumped and circled around her in excited greeting as she carried it to the side of the car. With a wide smile she overturned it. Several articles of clothing tumbled out. Suits, ties, shirts, socks. Still smiling, she gave the heap a couple of good solid kicks to spread things out.

Delighted, the dogs trampled over the clothes, sniffing and barking. Fred proved his recognition of Jared's scent by lifting his leg.

On the porch, four men watched in silence, with varying degrees of emotion.

Ah, Jared's favorite tie was snagged on her foot, she discovered. Eyes on his, she ground her heel into it.

Rafe grinned like a loon. Shane let out one full belly laugh. Devin watched in rapt admiration.

Jared just watched.

She wasn't finished. Not by a long shot. Back to the trunk she pulled out a leather-bound address book he'd left on the nightstand. Her smile cool, she held it open as if to demonstrate. Then tore the pages out and let them flutter onto the heap of the now dirty, dog-haired clothes.

She took out his shoes. The good Italian leather first. Holding them down for Ethel to sniff, Savannah let the first one fly, then the second, and the dogs gave grateful chase. Tennis shoes went next. Two pairs, one of which, she was delighted to note, was only two weeks old.

She hoped the dogs chewed them to shreds.

There was shaving gear to deal with. She pitched a piece here, a piece there, drawing out the event until Shane simply rolled out of his chair onto the deck of the porch, helpless with laughter.

But she'd saved the coup de grace. The wine.

There had only been one bottle open, but she'd tossed that before she left. She uncorked all three, all fine vintages, expensively French. Chin up, eyes challenging, she walked back to what was left of his clothes. She tilted her head first, darkly pleased when his eyes went to green slits. With a veteran waitress's skill, Savannah poured them out, all at once over his best suit.

Done, she let the bottles fall with a clink on the grass. Still without having uttered a word, she strolled back to the car, slid behind the wheel. With a final smile, an arrogant salute, she backed up, swung around and drove down the lane.

Other than Shane's helpless laughter, there wasn't a sound until Devin finally cleared his throat. He studied the mess on the lawn carefully, even patted Fred's head when the dog devotedly brought him one of Jared's mauled shoes.

"Well," he said at length. "I'd say she made her point, too."

"She's a spooky woman," Shane managed, mopping his streaming eyes. "I think I'm in love with her."

Because he knew what it was like to be at the mercy of his own heart, Rafe rose and slapped a hand on Jared's shoulder. "You know, Jare, you got two choices."

He was all but quivering with fury. "Which are?"

"Run like hell, or go get her. I know which one I'd choose."

* * *

Jared didn't do anything for a couple of hours. He knew himself well enough to understand that his temper could be dangerous. He worked off some steam, and worked up a sweat in the barn before washing up.

When he finally headed out, his anger was still there, but strapped in. She figured she was dumping him, he thought, like she'd dumped his things.

But she was going to figure again.

"Hey, Jare." From the side yard where he was playing tug-of-war with the dogs over one of Jared's shoes, Shane sent up a shout. "Tell Savannah we really enjoyed the show, okay?"

"Remind me to kick your butt later."

She'd humiliated him, he fumed. In front of his brothers. Seeking control, he jammed his hands into his pockets and veered toward the woods. Not to mention that she'd ruined a good portion of his wardrobe.

Thought she was damn clever, he was sure. He imagined she'd sat up half the night planning it all out. If he hadn't been the brunt of it, he'd have admired her finesse. The sheer nerve of it.

But he had been the one who took the brunt of it.

The woods closed around him, but he didn't experience the usual sense of peace and companionship. His mind was on the other side of them, on Savannah. And, he thought with relish, on revenge. Let's see how she liked it when he went into her closet and—

He stopped himself, took another deep breath. Look what the woman had brought him to. He was actually considering vandalizing her belongings in some sort of juvenile one-upmanship.

Wasn't going to happen. He would gain revenge by showing her that, despite her outrageous behavior, he was a reasonable man. To make certain he would be, Jared detoured off the path and sat down on the rocks.

He couldn't feel them—the ghosts that haunted this place with their sorrows and hopes and fears. Perhaps, he thought, because for the first time in a long time he was plagued with too many of his own.

He'd known loss. The jarring, devastating loss of his parents. He'd lived with that, because he didn't have a choice, and because, he thought, there were so many good, solid, important memories to draw on for comfort.

And, of course, he'd always had his brothers.

He'd known sorrow. He had been struck with it when he finally admitted his marriage had been a mistake.

Not a disaster. Somehow that would have been better, less pale, than a simple, easily rectifiable mistake.

Hope, of course. His life had been full of it, a gift from his parents, from his roots. Wherever there was hope there was fear, the price to be paid for the sweetness.

He'd known all those emotions, used them or overcome them. But until Savannah, he'd never known anything so sharp, so vital. So frightening.

The wind changed as he sat there, picked up, where it had been calm before. It fluttered the trees, whispered through the leaves that filtered sunlight. And chilled.

They came here. He sat very still as he thought of it. The two boys, wearing different colors, came here. Each of them wanted only to find home again. To escape from the madness into the recognizable. The familiar. To find the sense of it all again, the meaning of it. The continuity of family, of people who knew and loved them. Accepted them.

Maybe, in some odd way, that was what they'd fought for.

For home.

What an idiot he'd been, Jared realized, and closed his eyes as the wind scooped up dead leaves and swirled them around him. The two boys had never had a chance once they chose their path. But he had a chance. The same fate that had doomed those two soldiers so long ago had placed Savannah and Bryan right in front of him.

Instead of accepting, he'd questioned. Instead of rejoicing, he'd doubted.

Because what frightened him most was this blinding love. A love that demanded he protect, defend, treasure. And he couldn't protect the girl she had been, defend that girl against the cruel and thoughtless blows of life when no one else would help. She'd had to face it alone, without him. And, if necessary, she still could.

That left him feeling impotent, and scorched his pride.

So, he was an idiot. But she wasn't going to get rid of him easily.

He heard a rustling, and when he opened his eyes he wouldn't have been surprised to see a young Confederate soldier, bayonet ready, fear bright as the sun in his eyes, step off the path.

Instead, he saw Bryan, head down, feet scuffling leaves. He would have laughed at his overactive imagination if the boy's pose hadn't been one of such abject dejection.

"Hey, Ace, how's it going?"

Bryan's head came up. The smile, a bit more cautious than Jared was used to, fluttered around his mouth. "Hi. Just out walking. Mom's in a mood."

"I know." In an unspoken invitation, Jared patted the rock beside him. "She's pretty steamed at me."

"She said you were steamed at her, too."

"I guess I was." Instinctively Jared draped an arm over Bryan's shoulders when the boy settled beside him. "I'm over it. Mostly."

"She's not." Ready for male bonding, Bryan rolled his eyes. "She kicked me out."

"No, kidding? Me, too."

The idea of that had Bryan chuckling. He didn't think his mother had told Jared to go play outside, for God's sake. "We can go live at the farm, till she cools off."

"We could," Jared said consideringly. "Or I could go on over and try to smooth things out."

"Can you?"

Jared looked down, and for the first time saw the worry in the boy's eyes. "She's not really mad at you, Bry. She's mad at me."

"Yeah, I know. Can you make her not mad at you anymore?"

"I hope so. When you tick her off, does she stay that way long?"

"Nah. She can't, 'cause…" There was no way to explain it. "She just can't. But she's never let a guy hang around like you, so maybe she can stay mad at you."

"She's never…" He stopped himself. It was wrong to ask the child. "Maybe you should give me some pointers."

"Well." Bryan pursed his lips as he thought about it. "She really digs the flowers you bring her. No one ever did that before, except once I brought her some little ones for her birthday. She got all mushy about it."

"No one ever brought her flowers," Jared murmured. He wasn't just an idiot. He was a champion idiot.

"Nuh-uh," Bryan continued, warming up. "No one ever took us out to ball games or for pizza, and she likes that, too."

This time he could ask, because it was for the boy. "No one ever took you to ball games or for pizza?"

"Nah. I mean, Mom and me went, sure, but not with a guy who like set it up and stuff." Bryan was thinking that over, how much he liked it, when inspiration struck. "Oh, yeah. And when you're going to take her out, like on a date, she sings in the shower. She went out on dates before and all, but she never sang when she was getting ready. So maybe you should take her on a date. Girls like that stuff."

Jared determined there were going to be lots of ball games, lots of pizza, lots of dates and lots of flowers in Savannah and Bryan's future. "Yeah, they do."

"Have you got any love words?"

"Excuse me?"

"Like in the movies," Bryan explained. "You know how the woman gets all moon-eyed when the guy says love words. Only the guy has to be kind of moon-eyed, too, to make it work. She might like that."

"She might."

Bryan sighed at the thought. "It's probably embarrassing."

"Not if you mean them. Here's the thing, Bryan." Jared scooted away just enough that he could face the boy fully. "I figure I ought to run this by you, since you've been the man of the house for so long. I'm in love with your mother."

As his stomach clutched and jittered, Bryan lowered his gaze. "I kind of figured you were stuck on her."

"No, I'm in love with her. Moon-eyed. I'm going to ask her to marry me."

Bryan's gaze whipped back up, and this time it held steady and searching. "For real?"

"For very real. How does that fly with you?"

He wasn't ready to commit. Though he liked the strong weight of the arm on his shoulders, his stomach was still jumping. "Would you, like, live with us?"

"Not like. I would live with you, and you'd live with me. But there's a catch."

That was what he'd been afraid of. He braced himself, kept his eyes level. "Yeah? What?"

"I'm going to ask you to take my name, Bryan. And to take me on, as your father. I don't just want your mother, you see. I want both of you, so you both have to want me."

There was an odd pressure on his chest, as if someone had just sat on him. "You want to be my father?"

"Yes, very much. I know you've gotten along just fine without one up till now, and maybe I need you more than you need me, but I think I'd be good at it."

Bryan's eyes goggled. "You need to be my father?"

"I do," Jared murmured, realized he'd rarely spoken truer words. "I really do."

"I'd be Bryan MacKade?"

"That's the deal."

While he hesitated, Jared's universe simply ground to a halt. If the boy rejected him, he knew, it would cut straight to his heart.

But Bryan didn't know for sure how things were done between men. He knew what to do when his mother offered him something wonderful, something he'd hardly dared to dream of but had wished for hard, really hard, at night. So, in the end, that was what he did.

Jared found his arms full of boy.

The breath Jared had been holding whistled out in almost painful relief. Have a cigar, he thought giddily, you've got yourself a son.

"This is so cool," Bryan said, his voice muffled against Jared's chest. "I thought maybe you didn't want somebody else's kid."

Gently, for he suddenly felt very gentle, Jared cupped the boy's chin and lifted it. "You won't be somebody else's. We'd make it legal, but that's just a paper. What really counts is what's between you and me."

"I'll be Bryan MacKade. You'll make her go for it, won't you? You'll talk her into it?"

"Talk is my business."

Furious at herself for snapping at Bryan, Savannah ruined two illustrations before admitting that work was hopeless. She'd been so pleased with herself when she drove away from the MacKade farm. Drunk with the power of causing fury to run hot and cold over Jared's face.

Now she was miserable. Miserably angry, miserably frustrated. Miserable. She wanted to kick something, but wasn't so far gone she'd take it out on the two kittens napping in the corner of the kitchen.

She wanted to break something, but after a frustrated search through the living room she discovered she didn't have anything valuable enough to be satisfying.

She wanted to scream. But there was no one to scream at.

Until Jared strode through the door.

"You don't have so much as a cuff link left here, MacKade. Everything's in your front yard."

"I noticed. That was quite a show, Savannah."

"I enjoyed it." She crossed her arms, angled her chin. "Sue me."

"I might yet. Why don't we sit down?"

"Why don't you go to hell?" she drawled. "And be sure the door kicks you on your way out."

"Sit down," he repeated, in a tone just firm enough, just reasonable enough, to light a very short fuse.

"Don't you tell me what to do in my own house!" she shouted at him. "Don't you tell me what to do, period. I'm sick to death of you making me feel like some slow-witted backwater bimbo. I don't have a fancy degree—hell, I don't have a high school diploma—but I'm not stupid. I muddled through with my life just fine before you came along. And I'll do just fine after you've gone."

"I know." He acknowledged that with a slight inclination of his head. "That's what's been worrying me. And I don't think you're stupid, Savannah. On the contrary. I don't think I've ever met a smarter woman."

"Don't play that tune with me. I know what you think of me, and I can live up to most of it."

"I think you can," he said quietly. "I think you can live up to everything I think of you. If you'd sit down, I'll tell you what that is."

"I'll say what I have to say," she tossed back. "You want to know about me, Jared. I'll tell you about me. A parting gift, for all the good times. You sit down," she demanded, and stabbed a finger at a chair.

"All right. But this isn't why I'm here. I don't need to know—"

"You asked for it," she said, interrupting him smartly.

"By God, you'll get it. My mother died young, but she left my father and me first. She didn't go far, just across the corral, so to speak. Another smooth-talking cowboy. My father never got over it, never forgave, never gave an inch. Certainly not to me. He never loved me the way I wanted him to. He couldn't. Even if he'd tried, he couldn't. I wasn't a nice polite little girl. I grew up hard, and I liked it. Getting the picture?"

"Savannah, please sit down. You don't have to do this."

Enraged, she stalked over to him. "Listen. I haven't even gotten started, so you just shut up and listen. We didn't have much money. But then, a lot of people don't, and they get by. So did we. He liked to take risks, and he broke a lot of bones. There's more than manure on the rodeo circuit, more than sweat. There's desperation, too. But we got by. Things got a little interesting when I grew breasts. Men liked to stare at them, or sneak a feel. Most of the guys on the circuit had known me since I was a kid, so there wasn't much trouble. I knew when to smile and when to use my elbow. I was never innocent. The way I lived, you'd better grow up knowing."

He didn't interrupt now, but sat quietly, his eyes unreadable. And her hands were cold.

"I was sixteen when I took that tumble into the hay. I wasn't innocent, but I was a virgin. I knew, but I let myself forget, because... Because he was good-looking, exciting, charming, and, of course, he told me he'd take care of everything. No one had—"

"No one had ever taken care of you before," Jared murmured.

"That's right, and I was just young and stupid enough to believe him. But I knew what I was doing, knew the chance I was taking. So I got pregnant. He didn't want me or the baby. Neither did my father. I was just like my mother, cheap, easy. He told me to get out. He might have thought differently the next day. He had a quick temper. But I wasn't cheap, and I wasn't easy, and I wanted the baby. Nobody was going to take that baby away from me. Nobody was going to tell me to be ashamed. They tried. Social services, sheriffs, state cops. Whenever they could catch me, they tried. They wanted me in the system so they could tell me how to act, how to raise my child or, better for everyone, to give him away. But that wasn't better for me, and it wasn't better for Bryan."

"No. The system's flawed, Savannah. Overburdened. But it tries."

"I didn't need it." She lashed back at him. "I got work, and I worked hard. I waited tables, I served drinks, I cleaned up slop. It didn't matter what kind of work, as long as it paid. He never went hungry. My son never went hungry, and he always had a roof over his head. He always had me. He always knew I loved him and that he came first."

"The way you never did."

"The way I never did. Whatever it took, I was going to give him a decent life. If that meant taking off most of my clothes and dancing for a bunch of howling idiots, what difference did it make? I didn't have an education, I didn't have any skills. If I'd been able to go to art school—" She bit off the thought with a furious shake of her head.

"Is that what you wanted?" He kept his voice neutral, as he would have with a fragile or high-strung witness. "To go to art school."

"It doesn't matter."

"It does matter, Savannah."

"I wanted Bryan. Everything else was secondary. You wanted to know about men. There were a few. Scores less than you've imagined, I'm sure. I wasn't dead, just driven. I never took money from them, but I took food a couple of times, and there's not much difference. And, damn you, I'm not ashamed of it. The only reason I didn't steal was because if I'd been caught, they might have taken Bryan. But I would have stolen if I'd been sure I'd have gotten away with it. I didn't know I could peddle my paintings until one of the girls at the club asked me if I'd do one of her for her boyfriend and offered me a twenty. That's when I got the idea to take Bry to New Orleans."

She was pacing the room as she spoke, her words rushed and hurried in her effort to get them out and over. But now she stopped, slowed herself. "That's all there is. At least any other, finer details escape me at the moment." She turned to him again, her face calm now, and cold. "Cross-examine, Counselor?"

"You could have taken other routes."

"Sure."

"Safer ones," he added. "Easier ones, for you."

"Maybe. I didn't want safer ones. I didn't want easier."

"What did you want, Savannah? What do you want?"

"It doesn't matter."

"It matters." He rose, but didn't go to her. "It very much matters to me."

"I want a home. I want a place where people don't look at me like I'm dirt. Where the people who think they're decent don't whisper behind their hands."

"You have that here."

"And I'm keeping it."

He had to sacrifice his pride to ask, but he discovered it wasn't so very difficult. "Do you want me?"

Taken by surprise, she only stared for a moment. "That's not the issue."

"Then maybe I should put it another way." He reached into his pocket, drew out the small box he'd tucked in it before he left the farm. After lifting the lid, he held it out. "I came here to give this to you."

The ring was a simple, traditional diamond in an outdated and lovely gold setting. Mesmerized, Savannah gaped at it before slowly stepping back.

"It was my mother's," Jared said, in a voice that betrayed none of the raw nerves inside him. "It went to me, as I'm the oldest. I'm asking you to marry me, Savannah."

She couldn't breathe. Bryan would have recognized the weight that had dropped down on her chest. "Didn't you hear anything I've just told you?"

"Yes, everything, and I'm grateful you told me,

even under the circumstances. This way I can tell you I love what you were, what you are and what you will be. You're the only woman I've ever loved, and it's so amazing to find you admire someone as much as you love her."

She stepped back again, as if he were holding a gun instead of a promise. "I don't understand you. I don't understand you at all. Is this some sort of vicious payback because I ruined your clothes?"

"Savannah." His voice was patient now. "Look at me."

She did, and the weight on her chest doubled and pushed tears into her eyes. "Oh, God. You mean it."

"You're going to cry." He almost shuddered with relief. "Thank the Lord. I thought you were going to toss it in my face."

"I thought…you didn't think I was good enough for you."

The smile that had beamed onto his face froze. "Do I deserve that?" he murmured. "Sweet God, I hope not. I'm supposed to be good at making my case, but I've sure as hell screwed this one. I was afraid. It's hard for me to admit that. I'm a MacKade, and we're not supposed to be afraid of anything. I'm the oldest MacKade, and I'm supposed to be able to handle anything. But I couldn't handle how I feel for you. I was afraid of what was behind you, of what you wouldn't say to me. I thought it might explode in my face and ruin what I wanted to build with you and Bryan. And part of me was afraid—terrified, really—that you'd be able to toss me aside the way you did that photograph."

"Bryan." The weight on her chest dissolved like water. "You want Bryan?"

"Am I going to have to get down on my knees here?"

"No, don't." She wiped impatiently at the tears. "I couldn't handle it. I was worried that— It seemed that—"

"I wouldn't want him, because it wasn't me who rolled in the hay with you ten years ago? That wasn't it. Maybe it was part of it for a while. Pride gets in the way. What bothered me most is thinking of you being hurt, of the two of you scraping by. I can't help wanting to go back and save you, to protect you and Bryan. I can't help feeling, well, a little unmanned, really, because I can't go back. And because I know you don't need me to. And maybe it bothered me some that you'd managed to turn it all around into something admirable. You see, I wanted to take care of you, both of you, but you've done just fine without me."

"We'd do better with you."

Emotions trembled through him. Stepping forward, he laid a hand on her wet cheek. "That's the best thing you've ever said to me. That's the second incredible thing that's happened to me today."

She managed a smile. "There was another?"

"When I talked to Bryan in the woods. We were sitting on the rocks, where two lost boys met, trying to find their way home."

"It's a strong place."

"Yes. Not as sad after today as it once was. Bryan was giving me advice on how to coax you out of being mad at me. I was supposed to bring you flowers, which I will, and take you on a date, so that you could sing in the shower while you get ready."

She gave a watery, embarrassed chuckle. "He's got a big mouth."

"Then I'm supposed to come up with some love words, like in the movies. Girls like that stuff, I'm told."

"I guess I'm going to have to start keeping an eye on those girls. I'm glad you talked to him, Jared."

"That wasn't the best part. I told him I was going to

ask you to marry me and that I wanted to be his father. He hugged me," Jared murmured, struck by it all over again. "It was just that easy. He had a lot of faith that I'd be able to talk you into it. I hope I'm not going to disappoint him."

She did the simple thing and leaned into him, resting her head on his shoulder. "Before I answer the question, I'd better warn you. I don't believe in quiet, civilized divorces. If you try to worm out of this, I'll just have to kill you."

"Sounds fair, as long as it holds true for both sides." He turned his face into her hair, and knew he was home. "Ah, morning sickness and thirty-two hours of labor might put you off from trying again."

She squeezed her eyes tight, squeezed him tighter. He was offering her more children. He was offering her a future.

"Don't be an ass, MacKade. I'm tougher than that. And this time around I'd have someone to swear at in the delivery room."

"I want to be there for you, through everything. You're going to have to learn how to need me."

"Too late," she murmured. "I already know all about that."

"Take my name, Savannah. Take me."

"Savannah MacKade." Closing her eyes again, she held on tight. "I think it suits me just fine."

* * * * *

Mills & Boon® Online

Discover more romance at
www.millsandboon.co.uk

- **FREE** online reads
- **Books** up to one month before shops
- **Browse our books** before you buy

...and much more!

For exclusive competitions and instant updates:

 Like us on **facebook.com/romancehq**

 Follow us on **twitter.com/millsandboonuk**

 Join us on **community.millsandboon.co.uk**

Visit us Online   Sign up for our FREE eNewsletter at **www.millsandboon.co.uk**

WEB/M&B/RTL4

The World of Mills & Boon®

There's a Mills & Boon® series that's perfect for you. We publish ten series and, with new titles every month, you never have to wait long for your favourite to come along.

Blaze®
Scorching hot, sexy reads
4 new stories every month

By Request
Relive the romance with the best of the best
9 new stories every month

Cherish™
Romance to melt the heart every time
12 new stories every month

Desire™
Passionate and dramatic love stories
8 new stories every month

Have Your Say

You've just finished your book.
So what did you think?

We'd love to hear your thoughts on our
'Have your say' online panel
www.millsandboon.co.uk/haveyoursay

- 🌹 Easy to use
- 🌹 Short questionnaire
- 🌹 Chance to win Mills & Boon® goodies

Visit us Online Tell us what you thought of this book now at
www.millsandboon.co.uk/haveyoursay